FOR FORK'S SAKE

A RIVALS-TO-LOVERS ROMANCE

FARM 2 FORKING
BOOK 3

KAREN GREY

Published by HOME COOKED BOOKS

A division of Jasper Productions, LLC

Cover design © 2024 by Y'all. That Graphic.

First edition, July 2024

Content guidance for this book can be found at
www.karengrey.com/contentguidance

AUTHOR'S NOTE

For nearly a year, Lainey Davis, Liz Alden, Karen Grey, Erin Mallon, and Ember Leigh met weekly via Zoom to create a ridiculous, wonderful world: Fork Lick, New York. Each book in the Farm 2 Forking series represents a collaborative effort of forced extroversion, shared goat memes, and hot farrier TikTok analysis. Nothing has ever been more fun! Karen and Erin brought their theater backgrounds into the virtual writing room, while Lainey, Liz and Ember learned new ways to meld minds. They hope these books make you snort laugh, or at least take up knitting.

CHAPTER 1
DIANE

I KNEW IT WAS A BAD IDEA TO EAT IN THE HOTEL BAR, BUT THE adjoining restaurant had a half-hour wait, and I didn't feel like driving around looking for another place in the pouring rain. When the hostess pointed at an empty barstool and my stomach grumbled, I grabbed the spot.

Now, I wish I'd gotten my meal to go. Everything had been fine when I'd ordered dinner, but the moment the bartender set it in front of me, this creep slid into the open seat next to me. A man with no sense of personal space, who will not let me eat in peace.

"I said, no thank you," I repeat when he offers to buy me a drink. Again. My beer is only half-empty, and my appetite is gone. Where the hell did that bartender go? If I could just settle up, I could get out of here. Of course, then the guy might follow me to the elevator.

"You too good for me, is that it?" he asks, leaning even closer.

Wondering if I could get the hostess to help me out, I do my best to keep my voice even. "I'm not sur—"

"So sorry I'm late, honey," a warm, masculine voice says from behind me. "Who's your friend?"

Those rich tones would have me turning towards him like a flower to the sun even if there weren't a whiny asshole bothering me. When I do, I wish he *were* my honey. Thick, dark hair, chisel-cut cheekbones. Unruly brows, dark-rimmed glasses, pale blue eyes. So much like Henry Cavill's Clark Kent I'm wondering if he's got a superhero outfit under his tailored suit.

His eyes aren't just beautiful, they speak volumes. They're all guard-dog protective, until I arch a brow at him. When I get a glint of humor too, I decide to play along.

"I tried to save your seat, *sweetums*." My tone treacly sweet, I gesture at the man I've been saying *no* to in every way I know how for the past fifteen minutes. "But this man took it. And he won't leave me alone."

I swear Superman grows several inches in height as he slips between me and Won't Take No For An Answer Dude. "Are you bothering my wife, sir?"

Dude shrinks into his stool. "No, no, I was just, uh, making sure she was taken care of, you know."

"Kind of you, but as you can see, I've got it covered." Superman waits a beat and then tips his chin. "May I have my seat back?"

I swear the other guy goes boneless as he slithers off the bar stool. "It's all yours, my man."

"Thanks for keeping it warm for me," my hero says, the growl in his tone overriding the polite words.

Now more Clark Kent, my suited savior slips onto the vacated seat with the grace and agility of an athlete, eyes tracking the other man until he's well and truly gone.

When he finally turns back to me, even his grimace is attractive. "Sorry if that was presumptive, but if you were my sister, I'd have done the same."

As the words leave his mouth, he seems to realize what he's said, and he adjusts his glasses, almost nervously. "That sounded weird, huh?"

I nod slowly, hiding my amusement. What is it with him? I should be pissed that he stepped in, assuming that I'd need his help. Instead, I want to grab him by the lapels of his fancy suit and kiss him silly.

"It's just," he continues, his cheeks flushing pink. "I do have a sister—a twin—and I get super protective, especially when she gets that look on her face."

"The wide-eyed save-me look?"

"Exactly." He grimaces slightly. "Do you forgive me?"

I tip my head to the side as if I'm trying to decide. "I will if you tell me your name."

Relief has twin dimples appearing in his cheeks, and he holds out his hand to shake. "Samuel. Or Sam."

"Diane." His hand engulfs mine, and I have to force myself to release it. "I not only forgive you, I'm grateful. That guy would not go away."

The bartender finally returns, but instead of settling up and heading back to my room as planned, I offer to buy Samuel-Sam a drink. "What're you having?"

He tips his head to the side. "What were *you* having?"

I lift the half-full pint glass. "Chatham Farmer's Daughter. It's a local IPA. 'Spicy, fresh, and a little sassy' according to the menu."

"Sounds like my kind of girl." He nods to the bartender. "I'll take a Farmer's Daughter too."

Before I can ask if he indeed *has* a farmer's daughter—I

mean, I don't see a ring on his finger, but you never know —another man in a suit steps up behind us. "Sam, you forgot your portfolio."

Sam groans as he takes it and sets it down on the bar. "Thanks, John. As my grandma would say, I'd forget my head if it wasn't screwed on."

John's gaze immediately zeroes in on my breasts. "Who do we have—"

Before he can finish, Sam slaps him on the shoulder so hard that John stumbles slightly. "Thanks again. See you next week."

With a sleazy grin, John backs up. "Yeah, sure man. Got it. You got here first."

I swear Sam growls as he watches the man walk away, and when he turns back to me, he's frowning. "Can I just apologize for me and every other male out there?"

Laughing, I say, "Anytime."

He gestures at my half-finished meal. "Please, don't mind me. Eat."

I slump back in my seat. "I think I'm done."

"Which jerk ruined your appetite?"

"It's not them. This always happens with pasta at a restaurant. I can never get to the bottom of it. Plus, I'm a little nervous about a presentation I have to make tomorrow."

"Well, if you're not going to finish it, I will."

"Do you want a menu?"

"Nah." He hooks a thumb in the direction of the restaurant. "I had a work dinner, but I grew up with four siblings on my grandparents' farm. Hate to see food go to waste."

I slide the plate over and pepper him with questions about the farm. As he eats, I learn that they grow soybeans in the Catskills, and the farm's been in the family for generations.

"Do you work in agriculture?" he asks. "You seem to know a lot about it."

"I do." The reason I'm in this bar instead of holing up in my hotel room rears its head again. "I really don't feel like talking about work, though."

He lifts his beer. "Amen to that."

As the bartender refills his water glass, Sam asks for extra ice. I should ask for the check and head back to my room, but I've never been one to do what's expected of me. "How about a game instead? I'm obsessed with this new trivia app I found."

He narrows his eyes at me, and for the first time, I can't quite read him. "Which app?"

"It's called Trivia Crush."

He pulls his phone from his jacket pocket, unlocks it, swipes, and holds it up. "Hello. My name is Samuel. I'm a Trivia Crush-aholic."

The challenge in his blue eyes stokes a flame deep in my core—one that's been cold ashes of late. This could get interesting. Reminding my lady parts that I don't have the brain space for random hookups, I power up my app to ignite competitive engines instead. "This is exactly what I need. I usually play against this guy called Daniel12051 but—"

His beer glass hits the bar so hard liquid sloshes out of it. "What did you just say?"

"Um, that I usually play—"

"Daniel12051?"

"Uh-huh," I say, a little freaked out by the intensity of his voice.

He holds up his phone again. This time the app is open, and I can see his username emblazoned across the top. "That's me."

It's my turn to drop something. Luckily, Sam has quick reflexes and catches my phone before it hits the floor. When he places it in my palm, I think I might actually shudder.

"This is nuts," he says, his tone almost reverent. "You're Cortland1898. We've been going head-to-head for, what? Six months?"

I nod slowly. "Something like that."

The corners of his mouth lift in slow motion. When they hit a full-blown smile, I swear a tooth sparkles, like in a toothpaste commercial.

"Are we playing or what?" he asks, like I've been sitting here agog, jaw dropped, drooling, for five minutes. Which I probably have. "Or are you afraid you'll lose and it'll be too embarrassing?"

"Oh, no." Rallying, I literally shake myself, refusing to be derailed by mere physical attraction. Trivia is not trivial to this girl. "I won't lose."

He purses his lips momentarily—making me glad that I'm sitting down because otherwise I'd be a puddle on the floor—before saying, "Let's go."

Let's go, indeed.

It's just like when I'm playing Daniel12051 but in surround sound. Grunts of frustration when I beat him to an answer, roars of triumph when I get something wrong. I'm distracted enough by his scent—earthier than you'd expect given his buttoned-up look—that I don't dare look at him.

Per usual, I beat him at sports and literature. He crushes me in science. We go head-to-head with history and movies and music. Then he edges me out on the final bonus question, and I want to throw my phone across the room. "How the hell did you know that Taylor Swift song?"

But when I look up, the pure glee in those eyes melts all my frustration away. We're both suspended in that moment, leaning close, grinning like fools. His gaze flicks to my mouth, and I think he's going to kiss me. But then he blinks, shifts back, and stands abruptly.

Fumbling for his wallet, he slides a ten across the bar. "That was great, but I should turn in. Thanks for making my evening much better than it would have been."

He grabs the portfolio and is gone before I can try and say… what? *What's your last name? Where do you live? Can we see each other again?*

But as I'm signing the check, I notice his phone on the bar. Grabbing it and my purse, I sprint for the elevators. When I turn the corner, a tall, dark-haired man is about to step into a car. "Sam!"

He turns, a confused look on his face until he sees the phone I'm holding up. Knocking on his skull, he says, "That thing I said before about leaving my head behind? I wasn't kidding."

As I step closer, right in front of my eyes, he goes from golden retriever to German shepherd, searching the lobby. "Damn, I should've walked you to the elevator, just to make sure that jerk wasn't hanging around."

The lobby is practically empty, and we have the bank

of elevators to ourselves, but the minute I push the call button, the air shifts between us. When a car arrives and he ushers me in, it intensifies. It's a chemical thing, of course. His pheromones meet mine and want to party. I'm not one to deny myself simple pleasures, so the minute the doors slide closed, I face him. "How about a goodnight kiss as a concession prize?"

He frowns slightly, but he doesn't budge when I step closer. We're right back to that moment at the bar, but this time I'm not letting him get away without a taste. When our lips meet, the rest of my senses get on board, jumping in the deep end. The vibration under my feet tells me the elevator is going up, but I'd swear I'm in freefall. Hanging on to reality, I focus on what I feel. Strong fingers scrape my scalp and warm palms grip my jaw, tilting my head just so. The rough scrape of his five o'clock shadow contrasts with the downy softness at his nape. His musky scent is like rich loam ready for planting.

Suddenly, I'm parched by a thirst that could only be slaked by this tall drink of water. When the bell dings, we separate instinctively, panting like we just boxed a full round. The pull is elemental, but some part of my frontal lobe kicks in to operate my legs and feet and remove my hormone-drunk self from his orbit.

It's satisfying to see him look equally gob smacked as the elevator closes between us, but instead of strutting back to my room in triumph, I stare at the doors, second-guessing myself. Should I have asked him to join me? Or not have kissed him at all? A quiver of lust pings through me in answer.

Better to have kissed and lost than never to have kissed at all, as the poet said.

No use standing here in the hall letting the regrets pile up. Too late to change things. So I stumble in the direction of my room and dig for my key card.

CHAPTER 2
SAM

I'M NOT SURE HOW MANY FLOORS IT TAKES ME TO REALIZE that I missed mine. I'm not even sure what floor we were on when Diane stepped out of my arms. The only thing I'm completely sure of? I haven't taken a full breath since the doors closed between us. It feels like all the oxygen left when she did.

At some point, my hands take over, slapping the spots where I may have stashed my keycard. It probably wouldn't hurt to slap myself in the face, but before I can, I find the card, blessedly still snuggled inside the little envelope with my room number written on it.

Then I slap my face. That may have been the best kiss of my life. But I can't afford to take the relationship train right now. I don't have time to fall for a girl who will inevitably dump me. I'm not equipped to deal with the emotional fallout when I'm left alone, yet again, for being too much of a workaholic, too boring, too distracted, too absent-minded. You name it, I've had a girl break up with me for it.

Not that I've even been with that many women, but every single one has found some deal breaking habit or behavior that sends me packing, whether we've been together for a couple weeks or a couple years.

And I can't do one-night stands. I get too connected too fast, usually for the wrong reasons. I especially can't do a one-night stand *tonight*. My boss warned me that tomorrow's hearing will be boring as hell, so I need to get a good night's sleep if I'm to be on tap to answer any scientific or technical questions the state assembly members might have.

I keep up this mantra—adding in the fact that I don't know Diane's last name, let alone which room she's in, so seeing her again isn't going to happen no matter how much I wish I could—all while tossing my portfolio on the desk and shucking off my suit jacket. Even after I roll up my sleeves, the room is unbearably stuffy, so I crank up the AC, grab the ice bucket, almost leave without my keys —the number of times I've had to beg a desk clerk to give me another key because I've locked myself out is embarrassingly high—but remember at the last second, and then go looking for the ice machine.

I can see another person scooping ice through the small window, and when the door creaks, she looks over her shoulder. My eyes skip over the petite, brown-eyed beauty I never thought I'd see again, from the fine strand of honey-blonde hair draped over a freckled cheek to the plump lips surrounding an ice cube.

An entire X-rated movie flashes through my mind starring those lips, my dick, and all the other things we could do with a bucket of ice.

Diane sucks the ice into her mouth to ask, "You following me?"

I shake my head, "No, no, I promise, I—"

"Kidding." She grins, tipping her chin at my bucket. "Machine out on your floor?"

"No. Uh… this is my floor."

Her brows come together. "Then why didn't you get off the elevator when I did?"

I snort. "I had no idea where I was when you stopped that kiss. If you'd asked me the date, who the president is… heck, I doubt I'd have been able to tell you my middle name."

She tips her head to the side. "That was some kiss, huh?"

"How about another one?"

She presses her lips together and shakes her head. "I don't think so."

When I deflate, she laughs. "You kill me, Sam. I swear when you go from guard dog to defeated dog, you shrink six inches."

"You should see what else is shrinking." I adjust the ice bucket in my arms. "But I know how to take no for an answer."

She smiles and holds out her hand to make a little give it over motion. "Trade you. It took me forever to figure out how to get this guy to spit out the ice. Hate to see you waste all that time."

I hand over my bucket and watch as she does a little maneuver involving pressing a button while shoving the bucket under a dispenser before hip checking the hulk of a machine with a growl. Wondering if this is a dream, wondering if I could handle a one-night thing after all, I can't tear my eyes away from her.

"He's stubborn," she says, "but once you get him going, he gives it good."

Sounds like me.

"Oh really?"

Shit. I said that out loud.

"Yes you did."

I did it again.

"Still talking, buddy." She straightens, holding up the full bucket. "Was that a threat or a promise?"

"Uh… both?"

"You know," she says, tapping her chin with a finger, "the tragedy is, I only have one glass in my room."

I'm not sure where she's going with this, since she shut me down already. "Tragedy?"

"I can't invite you for a nightcap if I only have one glass."

"But you said you didn't want anoth—"

Ignoring my protest, she continues, her nose wrinkling adorably. "On top of that, they don't stock fridges with those cute little liquor bottles anymore."

My hand shoots into the air.

"Did you have something to share?" she asks.

I nod.

She's trying to hang on to this mock professor guise, but the glee underneath it zings between us. "Go ahead."

"I have two glasses and a gift basket with cute little liquor bottles. In my room," I add, in case it wasn't clear.

She tilts her head to the side. "Do you have your ID on you?"

"Uh, yeah. But I'm way over twenty-one."

Pretty sure she rolls her eyes, but she sticks out her hand. "Give it to me."

"My ID?" I ask, even as I pull out my wallet. She could ask for the keys to my car, my apartment, my soul, and I'd just hand them right over.

She peers at my driver's license briefly before taking a picture of it. "Sending this to a colleague I have to meet tomorrow in case I go missing, so don't try anything."

Before I can assure her that I'm harmless, she hands it back. "Twenty-eight was a good year for me."

"How old are you?"

"Thirty-one."

"How's that been?"

"My thirty-first year?" She grins. "I think it's about to get a little better."

"But you said no." Not wanting to assume anything, but needing another taste, I step closer.

"I said no to *just* another kiss," she says, speaking slowly and clearly so that even an emotional idiot like me can understand. "Because that would be maddening."

"Oh," is the only thing I can come up with in response. Luckily, my body has ideas of its own. Leaning in, I brush my lips behind her ear, and then drag them down her neck to the skin covering her taut trapezius, pausing to take it between my teeth briefly. When she gasps, I lave it with my tongue before shifting to find her eyes. "That okay?"

"Ye-yes." Shoving her phone in a pocket, she reaches up, probably intending to grasp the back of my neck, but she's got a long way to go.

"This'd be easier if we took these buckets and our

bodies back to your room," I suggest, in case she has second thoughts about coming to mine.

"*Your* room with the two glasses and cute bottles, and you're on."

"You sure?"

Her index finger skates across my clavicle, a fingernail circling the button at my sternum like she wants to pluck it off. "If we don't follow up on this, I'll be up all night wondering."

Taking that as a go, I usher her out the door and gesture in the direction of my room. Moments later, we're inside, and both buckets of ice land on the desk. Before I can offer her a drink, she says, "Wow, I thought I was messy."

Looking around the room, which is, indeed, a disaster area, I just shrug. "I've got a lot on my mind."

"Let's see if we can change that." Turning back to face me, she pulls her simple dress over her head, and her phone makes a muffled clunk when the fabric hits the floor. She's slim and wearing black scraps of lace that barely cover gentle curves my palms can't wait to caress.

"Well, that worked," I say, knocking on my skull. "Nothing left up here."

Without taking her eyes off me, she backs up until she hits the bed. "I hope you have enough brain cells left to strip."

My glasses, shirt, and trousers are off faster than I can answer. But before I can follow her across the bed, she calls, "Bring some of that ice, why don't you?"

After I plonk the bucket on the bedside table, I take a cube and trace a wet line down her abdomen. She arches into it, her skin pebbling, and I follow the trail with my tongue.

"Mmm, I like that. More."

"As you wish," I murmur, drawing a heart on her chest and a zigzag down her thigh. When she moans, I drag the rapidly diminishing cube back up her body. "Okay to get this pretty bra wet?"

She reaches behind her to unsnap it and whips it off, revealing teardrop shaped breasts with rosy nipples. I circle one, before sucking it between my lips, then I massage the other with the remains of the chip until the nipple glistens.

When I grab another chunk of ice and use it to trace her lips, she takes it from me. One hand pulls me in for a kiss, while the other slides the ice down my upper back. My own nipples harden, and I grind them into her breasts as my tongue revels in the chill of her lips contrasted with the warmth inside her mouth.

Her palm flattening on my back, her fingers fisting in my hair, she sucks on my tongue, and my dick feels like it's going to explode as I imagine thrusting into her pussy the way I'm thrusting into her mouth.

But first, the ice needs to tease her in another spot. Breaking the kiss, I grab a new cube and forge a path. Down her neck, straight through the cleavage, over her belly. Resting the ice in her belly button, I flatten my palm over it until she stops wiggling. Then, hooking my fingers around the fabric hugging her hips, I slide it down her legs, revealing trim curls.

Her chest rises and falls, her breasts tempting, but I've got important business to conduct. Retrieving what's left of the ice, I take it between my lips, spread her legs, and then prop myself up on my elbows. Releasing the ice with the same pop she'd made back at the machine, I spread the lips of her vulva too.

"So pretty," I say softly before playing over and around its folds until arching hips bring her bud to my lips. Chucking what's left of the ice over my shoulder, I dive in for a feast, exploring her with my mouth and fingers as I learn what she likes.

She's not shy about telling me, but I'm proud to say that she can't quite form a sentence. "More. There. Yes. Fuck," are the directions I get until her body goes rigid, she fists the sheets, and then finds her release.

I'm so fascinated with the way spasms roll through her entire body that her words take a moment to pierce the fog of my brain. "Sam. Condom? Please."

My brain scrambled, I lurch to the bathroom, praying that I'll find at least one in my dopp kit. The gods are with me. I have three. Grabbing them and a towel, I return to the bed where she's on her knees, still panting, making grabby hands. "Gimme."

I obey, handing over the packets, and shuck off my boxer briefs. Before I know it, she's got me sheathed and points to the bed. Falling onto it, I roll onto my back and let her take over the sweet torture of ice play until I can't take it anymore. "I need to be inside you."

As she mounts me, we gasp at the contact. She's slick and tight as hell. "I don't know how long I'm going to last."

With an evil grin, top teeth pressed to her reddened lower lip, she seats herself fully. Gripping my dick with the muscles of her vagina, she rises and falls, rolling her hips. So powerful. So beautiful. A goddess visiting earth just for me.

When she places my hands on her breasts and arches into them, my brain goes offline. All I can feel is the friction, the deep caverns of her, the tension spreading through every limb.

She gasps, her hips buck, her walls clench, and I flip her over, pistoning into her until I fall into complete oblivion.

Next thing I know, the sun's on my face, and there's a terrible sound coming from the bedside table. It takes me a minute to figure out that it's the hotel room phone.

As I reach for it, I realize that the other side of the bed is empty. Wondering if it's Diane inviting me to breakfast, I snatch it up. "Hello?"

"Where've you been?"

Unfortunately, the voice doesn't belong to Diane. It's my boss. Ron Lansdowne.

"Uh, here in my room. What's up?"

"I've been texting you for the past two hours."

Wondering if I'm late for the hearing, I check the clock, but it's only just past eight. Just as I'm wondering how early Diane left, a groan from Ron hooks my attention.

"I think I have food poisoning," my boss says, his voice hoarse. "You're going to have to do the hearing solo."

"By myself? But I—"

"Oh shit. Hang on." The phone clunks, and I hear him mutter, "I knew it was a bad idea to order shrimp."

Do the hearing solo? I've never even been to one of these

things before, and now I have to argue in support of new state regulation, representing not just my company but the entire Seed Trade Association?

I'm up and out of bed and pacing as far as the cord will allow, my own gut churning, when Ron begins talking again. No preamble, he barks orders. "I emailed my statement and some additional talking points to you. Take a look at them and call me on my cell if you have any questions. Ugh. I gotta go again."

"But Ron—"

"You do well, I'll push for an early promotion."

And then he's gone, replaced by the dial tone. Dropping the receiver in the cradle, I scrub a hand through my hair, trying to figure out what to do first.

Grabbing my cell phone, I stare at it, wondering why the hell I didn't get Diane's number. Or her last name, even.

But then Ron's words come back to me. *Early promotion.* The more money I make, the sooner I can leave this horrible job behind.

I need coffee and a shower before I can digest any of this. Twenty minutes later, I'm back in a suit. Weather app says it's decent out—for November in Albany anyway—so I walk to the New York State Assembly building instead of calling an Uber. The bright blue sky and brisk breeze clear my head, but it's not enough to calm my nerves.

Or my conscience.

It's bad enough that Congento sues farmers who accidentally grow our seeds because they blew over from a client's farm. But to stamp out something as harmless as a seed library or co-op that's likely doing actual good for the world?

I manage to find the hearing room and a seat before the politicians arrive, so I hunker down to reread the email Ron sent. As I do, I'm wondering if I have food poisoning too, or if the nausea is coming from the thought of saying this particular brand of fake news out loud, when someone nudges my shoulder.

I grew up with three brothers, so I instinctively swat the hand away.

"Ouch! What the hell, Sam?" a woman yelps.

I look up to find Ron's assistant Marianne glaring at me. "Uh, what are you doing here?"

"Bringing you these." She hands me a stack of papers and points to the raised bank of desks where the state representatives on the agriculture committee are now getting seated. "You have to provide copies of your testimony." She checks her watch. "I need to rearrange Ron's schedule for the day. You good?"

No fucking way am I good, is what I want to say, but an image of my grandfather's proud face when I told him about landing this job has me sucking it up. "Yeah. I've got what I need."

Moments later, a man introduces himself as the chair of the NYSA Standing Committee on Agriculture. "I hereby call this public hearing to order, where our invited guests will articulate their concerns and/or support regarding SB 385, which regulates the practices of seed sharing, libraries, and banks. Please remember to keep your statements under three minutes."

Thankfully, a few other citizens are called to testify before me, so I get to see the routine. Take your place at the desk facing the lineup of the committee members, hand over the stack of paper to an aide, read your statement into the microphone, and then answer questions. I'm scrolling through Ron's words on my phone, wondering if I can say them aloud without throwing up, when the guy next to me points at the name on the lanyard around my neck. "I think they're talking to you."

Blinking, I take the stand. Words march across the screen and out of my mouth into the microphone. Words that belie everything I learned in school. Words that don't even make logical sense. When I want to scream that it's all lies, I remind myself of how proud my grandfather was when I told him about landing this job. He actually patted me on the back, saying that he knew his investment in me would pay off. "Maybe you'll use that big brain of yours to invent a soybean that'll make me rich."

So I keep reading. "The Seed Trade Association would like to remind the assembly that unregulated seed distribution is a potential threat to our state's—even our country's—food system. Without regulation, including state-monitored testing, there's nothing to stop bad actors from infiltrating these groups and introducing contaminants into the food supply."

Before I can continue, one of the representatives asks, "Let me make sure I'm getting this right, Mr. Lansdowne. Are you saying that there's a threat of some sort of agroterrorism?"

I'm so shocked at the word that I don't bother correcting him about my name. Looking at my notes, I continue reading. "Uh, what I'm saying is laws governing the distribution of seeds, like any truth in labeling laws, protect the livelihoods of farmers who need to be able to trust the quality of the seeds they're working with and prevent unfair competition between seed purveyors."

A different representative calls for the floor. "Does the Seed Trade Association believe that seed libraries and seed banks are essentially and legally analogous to seed companies like Congento?"

The chair, thankfully, interrupts me. "He's not here to testify on that subject, Assembly Member Tanner. He's here to talk about the potential dangers associated with lack of regulation or testing of seeds."

Just when I think I'm off the hook, another representative is called on. "Would you say, Mr. Lansdowne, that libraries sharing seeds–this agroterrorist scenario–makes our food system vulnerable?" Pulling her microphone closer to her mouth, she adds, "The way we need to control the pornography librarians are selling to our vulnerable children?"

My sister Colleen would kill me if she heard this.

When they run out of follow-up questions, I'm relieved to be dismissed, hoping I did enough to keep my job without completely selling my soul. If you're going to sacrifice your integrity on the altar of Big Agro, it'd better be worth it.

I gather my things and stumble back to the general seating of the hearing room, wondering how long I have to stick around. Just as I drop into my seat, a familiar voice echoes through the room.

"On behalf of the Hudson Valley Seed Alliance, I thank the chair and committee for inviting me to testify today with my concerns regarding State Bill 345."

What the actual fuck? The woman who, just hours ago, called out my name in passion is now speaking into the microphone. Just when I hope I'm hallucinating, Diane finds my face in the crowd and sends me a look that guts me. I may not be great at reading people, but that lip curl combined with a slow shake of the head clearly communicates what I deserve: her disgust.

I drop into the nearest seat, heart in my throat, and watch as she turns back to the assembly, straightens the stack of notes in front of her, and then testifies without even glancing at them, as ardent on the stand as she was in my bed. "The only entities seed libraries threaten are conglomerates like those who make up the Seed Trade Association. Farmers and gardeners saving and sharing seeds, doing the work to preserve local varieties, protects our food systems by making us more resilient."

She continues with a series of well-thought-out arguments regarding the value of seed libraries, all of which I personally agree with—how they can be a center to a rural community, helping those in need to grow their own food and generally contributing to self-sufficiency.

Unfortunately, a few of the representatives won't stop badgering her about the dangers I brought up.

"I just don't understand why you'd be against testing and regulating seeds. What are you trying to hide?"

"It's not a matter of hiding anything," she replies, an impatient edge sharpening her voice. "It's a matter of scale. A library or bank is never going to collect enough seeds in a given year to amass the sample size sufficient for proper testing. Not to mention the fact that even if there were a contaminant present, twenty seeds shared from one farmer to another wouldn't have the impact that ten thousand contaminated seeds sold by a corporation would."

"So you're admitting that some sort of infiltration of

infected seeds by an agroterrorist is possible?" the representative asks.

Diane's pale cheeks redden, and her entire torso tenses up. "The vertical integration that the conglomerates running the Seed Trade Association have achieved gives them dangerous control over our nation's food production." As her voice rises, the microphone shrieks, making people flinch.

"Please control yourself, miss," the chairman drones, making me wonder why he calls her miss while he called me Mr. Lansdowne.

She clears her throat and takes a sip of water before continuing. "Laws like the one being proposed would actually make us more vulnerable to the rapid shifts wrought by climate change, whereas seed saving allows us to conserve local and disappearing plant varieties, not be forced to buy them year over year from"—she breaks off to shoot me another lethal glare—"from corporations primarily focused on shareholder profits."

The chair gives the floor to a different assembly member, who circles back to ask again why Diane's group is so against regulation. "Don't you realize that every state in the country requires seed companies to be licensed and to test and label all their products?"

"Of course, I realize that." At her words, the mic makes the awful sound again, and she shifts to speak around it. "But in many states, those laws only apply if you're selling seed, not trading or sharing them."

"Well, who's to say what selling is? Bartering is an exchange, after all. Just because money isn't involved… I think it's a legal gray area."

Before Diane can rebut this idea, the chair dismisses

her. After she thanks them, she uses the walk back to her seat to find my face in the crowd. I begin to stand, but she stops me with a slow shake of her head, like she can't believe she let me touch her, let alone have sex with her. Like I'm something she just wants to scrape off the bottom of her shoe.

Kind of how I'm feeling about myself right now. I went to Cornell's ag school because I wanted to learn how to save family farms. I may be making enough money to help support my family farm, but the work I'm doing destroys small farms.

And I just don't think I can do it anymore. Thinking that I might be able to explain all this to Diane, I scan the room for her face. When I don't find it, I head for the exit, but she's not in the hall either. Before I can look further, my phone vibrates. My boss's name flashes on the screen. Even though I'm not sure what I'll say, I answer.

"Great job, Sam. You didn't look nervous at all, while that girl—you really rattled her. She was practically hysterical."

"She had valid points, Ron."

"Trust me, it'll be that sound bite about agroterrorism and her red face that make the news."

"Like we really need to be squashing seed libraries."

"Goliath got taken down by David, don't forget. Meaning: We squash the opposition whenever and however we can."

David and Goliath. Whose side am I really on? The conglomerate's or the farmer's?

"They're coming for your job, you know," Ron continues.

"You know what? They can have it. I quit."

I hang up before I can second-guess myself. My gut tightens, remembering how proud Grandad was when I got the offer from Congento. From his perspective, they're what makes his soybean farm successful.

It's been nice to have a company car and a big expense budget so I can take clients out to fancy restaurants where I explain Congento's innovations in layman's terms, innovations that are impressive from a purely scientific standpoint. But Diane articulated the essential truths. Congento is about making money for its shareholders, not about farmers. Or even food.

Determined to find her and ask forgiveness, I search up and down the hallway. I even return to the hearing room and scan every seat, but there's no sign of her. Back outside, I stare at my phone like it might cough up her number, but I didn't have a chance to get it.

But I do have Trivia Crush. Opening the app, I search for user Cortland1898. In the past, every time I've invited her to play, I'd get a zing of anticipation. Now, there's a whole new level of excitement. But instead of a message that she's either ready to play or offline, there's a big red slash across her avatar.

She's blocked me.

Getting dumped by women is kind of my thing. I mean, I don't blame them. I'm a workaholic, I get tunnel vision, I forget dates, I'm boring. Friends and family call me a player because I cycle through relationships so fast, but ninety-nine point nine percent of the time, I'm the one who got left dangling in the wind.

But even though I've known this woman for less than twenty-four hours, the connection I felt with her was different. Deeper.

The disgust and dismay in her eyes were the final nail in the coffin for this job. I need to be a better man, even if it's too late for her to see it.

Quit your job, lose the girl, what else could go wrong?

Then I remember. It's almost Thanksgiving. I've promised to visit my grandparents' farm for the holiday. I won't be able to hide this news if I'm there in person. I'll have to tell my grandfather.

Diane isn't the only one who'll be disappointed in me.

CHAPTER 3
DIANE

Seven Months Later

When I turn off the county road and onto the tree-lined driveway of Bedd Fellows Farm, my tires crunching on the gravel, the sun peeks out between the clouds, and I'm tempted to pull over and start shooting B-roll. The property owners have already signed releases online, and the perfectly aligned rows of bright green soybean plants covering the rolling hills on either side of me glisten from recent showers like they're preening for the camera.

If I stop, I'll be late, so I make myself continue up the drive. Over the final rise, I'm rewarded with the sight of a picture-perfect gabled farmhouse. Slowing my approach, I tuck away the combination of nerves and anticipation that's been buzzing through me all morning. I'm finally starting to get comfortable with my equipment, but this video business is all still pretty new. I love meeting new people and talking to them, but it's nice to have a personal connection at Bedd Fellows. You never know what you're going to find when you roll up to meet a new interview subject.

Like the old guy who was, unfortunately, as stinky as he was knowledgeable about heirloom peas. Or the woman who aimed a shotgun at me until she remembered that she'd invited me to her property. Mostly, though, I'm heartily welcomed by people eager to share their stories.

Colleen Bedd and I were both members of Vassar SEED —Students for Equitable Environmental Decisions— though she was a few years behind me. When we reconnected at an alum event a few weeks ago and she heard about my new project, she invited me to visit, thinking I might like to interview her grandmother.

Lost in thought, I have to slam on the brakes to avoid hitting a sheep that's appeared in the middle of the driveway. I'm practically at the house, and the sheep doesn't look like it's going anywhere, so I just put my car in park and get out.

"Hi there… sheepie," I say, looking around for a dog. I'm almost always greeted or warned off by a farm dog, but maybe the sheep is this home's guard animal?

I don't know if sheep can be aggressive, so I take the long way around the car, grabbing my smaller equipment bag in case Mrs. Bedd wants to jump right in on the interview. Since I started my YouTube channel "Seeds of Change," I've learned that people usually share the most interesting tidbits before things get official.

The front steps creak as I mount them, but it's a gorgeous old place. Classic white clapboard with black trim, it's got a wide, wraparound porch, welcoming rocking chairs, and a swing nestled between planters. But it's the building next to the house that catches my attention. Curious, I drift past the picture window to check it out. Is it a playhouse? A fancy tool shed?

"It's quite the spectacle, huh?" Colleen asks from behind me.

"Oh!" Whipping around, I just manage to save my equipment from spilling out of my bag.

"Sorry to scare you," Colleen says with a sly grin, not looking terribly sorry.

Hand to chest, I let out a breath. "I shouldn't have been snooping. I just couldn't help—" Breaking off, I wave a hand at the side building. "Did you play there when you were a kid?"

Colleen shakes her head. "Nah, it's only five or six years old."

She doesn't provide further clues, so I ask. "For the grandchildren, then?"

"Nope." I didn't spend a lot of time hanging out with Colleen at school, but I can read the hint of mischief in her eyes. She's fucking with me.

"Ah, so it's a…" I cast my gaze across the yard, looking for the most ridiculous possibility, and it lands on the animal still parked in front of my car, still chewing its cud, or whatever sheep do. "House for the sheep?"

Colleen snorts. "Wow. Nobody ever guesses that fast."

"Riiight." Now I *know* she's screwing with me. "I wasn't born yesterday, you know."

She just shrugs, holding back a smile. "My grandparents had a special relationship."

Not sure I want to know what *that* means, especially with regards to the sheep, I remember she told me of her grandfather's passing at the end of last year. "I'm so sorry for your loss."

"Thanks. It's been tough." She sighs, and the energy

seems to drain out of her. "Come on and meet Gran. She's in the garden."

"The light is perfect right now. Okay if I start filming?"

Colleen shrugs. "Fine with me."

She leads me around the side of the house, past the building where the sheep supposedly lives, and beyond an impressive compost pile before stopping at a gate. Colleen nods at the tall fence as she opens it. "We have a lot of deer."

I almost feel like I'm entering the Secret Garden as I follow her through the gate. It's not a fussy, formal place with mazes and roses, but it is beautifully laid out. Well-kept plots burst with produce: summer squashes, pole beans and cucumber. Tomatoes as big as your head and as small as a thimble.

Speechless, I take my time weaving up and down rows, zooming in on a yellow and green striped melon here, following a bee as it pollinates a zucchini blossom there.

"I'm sure the birds and the bees have plenty to say about seeds. If only you knew their language," a woman with a slightly raspy voice says from behind me.

Turning, I find a grandma straight out of central casting grinning at me... until she sees the phone I've instinctively aimed at her. "We starting this already? But I haven't done my makeup!"

She's got me going for a few beats, and then I see the same exact expression Colleen beamed at me when she tried to convince me that the sheep lived in that monstrosity next to the house. Rolling my eyes, I grin. "You got me."

"If you can't laugh at life, then it's not worth living is what I say." Mrs. Bedd flicks a hand at my phone. "You can point that thing at me if you want. Hopefully I won't break it."

"I was just trying to catch your gorgeous garden at magic hour, but my mother did teach me some manners." She, in fact, instilled in me an endless list of proper behavior, but I won't go into that. "Nice to meet you, Mrs. Bedd. I'm Diane McCarthy, a college classmate of Colleen's."

"Call me Ethel, honey," Mrs. Bedd says, her grip firm as she squeezes my hand and then brushes it off. "Whoops, I got you dirty there."

"Part and parcel of interviewing farmers." I nod at the basket of vegetables under her arm. "If it's okay, I'll just film while you finish up whatever you're doing."

"That's good, because I have to get the tomatoes in. We're supposed to have a big storm tonight, and I don't want them to get busted up. Colleen, can you fetch those bushel baskets? I need you to pitch in."

"Yes, ma'am." Colleen disappears, and Ethel sets to work, efficiently palming and twisting tomatoes off vines before nestling them into her basket.

"Be sure to get the ones just starting to turn too, Colleen," Ethel says. Holding up a tomato that's mostly green to the camera, she adds, "Most tomatoes will ripen in the sun on the counter or windowsill. Harvesting them before they're fully ripe means I get 'em before the bugs and birds do."

Ethel is a natural on camera, so I just keep asking questions. "Can you tell me about these varieties? They're beautiful."

"They are, aren't they?"

She recites each variety's name, qualities and origin as she moves down the row. "Every one of these tomatoes grew from seeds saved by one of the gals in my knitting group. All regional heirlooms. Some of 'em passed down for generations."

Breathless as my camera records what is, essentially, food porn, I can't wait to upload it to my computer so I can share this beauty with the world. As I often do when I get excited about a video, I send a silent thanks to the jerk who nudged me in this direction. We may have shared a night of sex that I revisit all too often when I'm alone in bed with a vibrator, but it was his testimony in front of the commission that spurred me to start Seeds of Change.

It was far too easy for him to feed the members of the committee nonsense they ate right up. To make them believe that seed savers are some sort of food terrorists. Meanwhile, their eyes glazed over at the very real statistics I shared regarding the loss of biodiversity in agriculture.

In that moment, I realized I needed to take my message to the streets. To teach as many people as possible that nurturing locally grown food is necessary for our survival as a species.

I may have been hurt by his deception, but I was angry too. Angry at him, but even more angry at my family. After all, it was our shameful legacy that propelled me to start the seed library in the first place. But after the hearing last year, fueled by the need to undo the damage my grandfather set in motion, I dug out my notes from documentary classes I took in college, studied other farming YouTube channels to make sure I wasn't reinventing a wheel, put everything but the essentials in storage, moved out of my apartment, and hit the road.

If I ever see that guy again, I'll want to slap him. But I should probably thank him first.

CHAPTER 4
DIANE

WITHOUT EVEN TRYING, I END UP WITH A LUNCH INVITATION and continue to film Ethel as she effortlessly whips up a meal for a hungry crowd like it's her mission in life. Without batting an eye, she welcomes each new arrival into the fold and makes them feel at home by giving them a job to do.

"My husband and I were only able to have one child, so when our grandchildren came to live with us, I had to learn how to stretch a meal real quick. After all, I had five growing kids to feed, plus half of their friends too," Ethel grins as she pulls jars from the fridge. "I don't get to do it as often these days, but when Lia and Molly said they wanted to go over some things for tomorrow's strawberry picking, I said I'd make lunch for everyone."

First, a petite redhead stops in with fresh eggs and milk. Ethel sets her up beating eggs next to Colleen, who slices some of the tomatoes harvested earlier. And just before the skies open up with the predicted thunderstorm, a tall man who looks slightly familiar ushers in a beautiful brunette. As they enter, the woman lifts a cloth from the basket she's carrying. "Brought my latest batch of gluten-free sourdough rolls."

As Colleen introduces me, she explains that her older brother Ethan runs the family soybean operation, the brunette is his girlfriend Lia, and the redhead, Molly, works at a dairy farm down the road as well as at the Bedd's weekend strawberry picking operation. I've suddenly got ideas for new videos, from the challenges facing field crop producers like Ethan to the added value of pick-your-own offerings. The subjects are outside the scope of my original purpose for the channel, but as I meet more and more people and learn about the trials growers go through, it feels right to keep listening.

There's something about this family too. The way they treat each other—whether they're a blood relation or not—is a complete one-eighty from the way I was brought up, and I just want to spend more time with them and soak it all in.

I put my camera away when we gather around the table. Everyone dives into the simple but amazing meal: ham, goat cheese and herb frittata with pickled vegetables and Lia's rolls on the side. I can only imagine the way my mother would turn up her nose at the menu, but it's not like she actually eats. She'll do everything in her power to get a reservation at a Manhattan restaurant just because everyone's talking about the chef, and then only eat two bites of her meal.

Once everyone's been served, Colleen turns the tables on me. "What prompted you to start a YouTube channel? Didn't you study something to do with sustainable development?"

"I did, but I minored in communications. After I graduated, I went to work at a non-profit focused on seed libraries." *Went to work* is what I always say because people treat you differently if you tell them you funded a nonprofit with your trust fund. "We ran into some roadblocks at the end of last year when the state passed new regulations on sharing seeds."

"I remember that," Ethel says. "Some of my friends got skittish about sharing seeds in public because they didn't want to get fined. Did the nonprofit fold?"

"Oh, it's still going. And our advocacy helped to get the laws altered. But I pivoted to doing evangelical work."

A few utensils clatter, all other conversation stops, and everyone stares at me.

Finally, Colleen clears her throat. "Do you mean, like, selling Bibles? We're not, uh, religious."

"Oh, not that kind of gospel. I'm spreading the word of local varieties, like your grandmother's strawberries. At first, I just wanted to give farmers a platform, but it's really taken off. I'm raising money, learning, and teaching all at the same time."

"Do you ask for money?" Lia asks.

"I do link to the nonprofit, but I also make money from ads." I waggle my eyebrows. "Throw in enough shots of shirtless farmers, and people will listen to anything, turns out. Hashtag FarmPorn for the win."

Ethel makes a noise, and I worry that I've offended her, but when I catch her eye, it's twinkling with humor as she points a fork at Ethan. "I've got three other handsome grandsons besides the one at the table."

Colleen snorts. "Maybe you can"—she breaks off to make air quotes—"'interview' all four of them."

Ethan rolls his eyes, but his girlfriend claps her hands. "I vote for that!"

"Are they all farmers?" I ask.

"Two of us are," Ethan says. "Besides me, Alex manages Udderly Creamy down the road."

I point to the now-empty frittata pan. "Let me guess: the milk and eggs are from there?"

"Yes." Molly grips my arm, drawing all of my attention. "Diane, they have baby goats. Baby. Goats."

"Aw," I say. "I bet they're cute."

She leans into me, face serious but a twinkle in her eye. "They are beyond cute. They will melt your viewers' brains. Brace yourself." With a flash of a grin, she lets my arm go.

"That is tempting," I say, going over my upcoming schedule in my head and wondering if I can make some adjustments so I can stay longer.

"You really should get a look at what Ethel's got going on in the basement," Lia says. "With the innovations she's come up with–"

"Ethan perfected them," Ethel cuts in.

"It was a collaboration," Ethan concedes.

"Anyway," Lia says, with a quick kiss on the cheek to Ethan, making the burly farmer blush. "The amount and variety of food she's able to grow in a single season is truly astounding. And that's all due to what she's got going on down there."

Raising my brows, I look over at Ethel.

"This basement sounds like a must-see."

She waves a hand in the air. "I'd planned to take you down there after lunch, don't worry."

"Plus we've got a slew of local vendors coming

tomorrow to sell their wares to the folks that come to pick strawberries," Molly says. "There's a woman who sells honey, a potter, a guy who makes organic pet treats… it's a fun variety."

"Any of those baby goats coming?" I ask. "That'd get me there, for sure."

"Nooo…" Molly taps the tip of her nose with a finger. "But I like how you think."

"Where are you staying?" Colleen asks. "You don't live nearby, do you?"

"I'm a bit of a rolling stone at the moment, going wherever the next interview takes me. Sometimes I camp out of my car, sometimes I find a hotel."

"You won't find a hotel in Fork Lick," Lia says. "You'd have to get to Climax for that."

My expression must reveal my confusion because Colleen laughs. "Climax is the nearest real town. Not, you know, that kind of climax."

"R-right. Of course," I stammer, almost knocking over my water glass as I reach for a drink, hoping to cool my heated cheeks. "I think I saw it on the map."

Before I can ask if they have any recommendations, Molly peppers me with questions about my camping experiences and tells me all about her tricked-out van.

"Vanlife is definitely outside of my channel's purview, but I'd love a tour."

"You're welcome to stay here," Ethel says. "We've got plenty of room."

I meet Ethel's gaze. "Oh, thank you, but I don't want to impose."

"The attic bedroom is empty," she says. "We'd love to have you."

Secretly happy to get to spend more time with this fun-loving family, I gratefully accept the invitation. "What about your other two grandsons? I'm guessing they don't live at home since you've got so many available bedrooms."

"The youngest, Jackson, is some kind of music genius," Ethel says, her eyes shining with pride. "He's in a rock band. He's on the Spotify and everything."

"Wait." I grab Colleen's wrist. "Jackson Bedd is your brother? How did I not know this?"

Colleen scoffs. "First of all, he wasn't 'Jackson Bedd Superstar' when we were in college. He was just my annoying little brother."

Deciding it's best to not dwell on the celebrity, even though an interview with him would be amazing, I ask, "And the other one?"

"That's my twin, Sam," Colleen says.

Sam. I can't stop the memories that flash through my mind. Through my entire body. The best night of my life followed by the worst morning. When I fell for the enemy. When I realize everyone is staring at me, I muster the manners drilled into me. "What does Sam do?"

"He's an extension agent. He's been working in the western part of the state, so he hasn't been around much."

So it can't be the same guy. *My* Sam was a suit working for the enemy. He couldn't be a member of this family, anyway. One, it would be too crazy of a coincidence. Two, they're much too nice. Three, his last name is Lansdowne.

Funny thing is, I'm not sure whether I should be relieved, or disappointed.

After lunch, once the kitchen's spick and span, I follow Ethel down to the basement. The stairwell is horror-film creepy, but once we turn the corner and she flicks on the lights, I feel like I'm in a whole other movie: *The Martian*.

Hopefully, minus the human poop fertilizer.

"Wow," is all I can say, half expecting to see Matt Damon peek out from behind one of the racks. Wishing I had my camera, I whip out my phone instead. Without setting up a lighting or anything, I start filming. "Tell me about what all you've got going on down here, Ethel."

"Let's start at the end, shall we?"

She flicks on another light, and I follow her past shelves tricked out with grow lights to the other side of the basement where, like Vanna White in a stained apron and sturdy shoes, she gestures at row upon row of jars stuffed with fruits and vegetables in every color of the rainbow.

"This is going to make people go nuts. Jars in kitchen pantries are all the rage these days."

"What goes around comes around, I guess. I've had some of these jars for twenty or thirty years. Get 'em in bulk at the Feed n' Seed or the Price Chopper if I need to restock—which, come to think of it, I'll have to do soon since we're selling more than trading this summer."

She pulls a tiny little spiral notebook and stub of a pencil from her apron pocket and makes a note. Next, she shows me her pickling and canning set up: a cooktop and sink, a freestanding stainless-steel counter piled with cutting boards, utensils and pots hanging overhead. "We use every bit of what we grow. If I'm not canning it, I freeze it. If we can't eat it, we compost it." She points to a freezer and a garbage can in turn.

Walking back toward the stairs, she points at one of the racks filled with seedling trays. "This is where my starts acclimate before we take them outside. These are the autumn varietal strawberries you were asking about. We're planting them this week."

Pointing at a roll of plastic, she adds, "In the winter, we wrap the racks and turn them into little greenhouses."

Looking around the efficiently laid out basement work-space, where Ethel seems to literally take food from seed to table, I ask, "What made you think to do all this?"

"I saw something like it on YouTube." She leans on the central table, tapping its surface. "At first I was only growing down here, but then I figured out that it's also the perfect place to dry seeds. We just run the dehumidifier." After tipping her chin toward the machine humming in the corner, she lifts a paper towel covering a metal baking tray. "These are from early summer crops."

"It all comes full circle down here," I say as I shoot a closeup of the tray of seeds. "It's beautiful."

Not only is it beautiful, but Ethel is the most progressive farmer I've met of her generation, and it makes me wonder how much input she has in the soybean operation, which seems more conventional. We're too busy to delve into these questions, however. I spend the next hour toggling between shooting footage and jotting down Ethel's many ideas for videos, which include people to interview as well as topics that hadn't occurred to me. From a neighbor who's growing black cohosh—"I wouldn't have made it through menopause without her tinctures"—to another who grows twenty different varieties of winter squash, some I've heard of, like Hubbard and Spaghetti and others that I can't wait to see, like Cinderella and Honey Bear.

By the time we wrap, I'm convinced. "If you're sure it's not an imposition, I'd love to stay. For another few days at least."

"I'm so happy to hear it." Ethel clasps her hands in front of her soft bosom, her smile lifting her cheeks into bright pink apples reminiscent of my own grandmother's crops. "Let me show you your room."

CHAPTER 5
SAM

AFTER SPENDING THE MORNING TOURING THE UPPER HUDSON Valley Cooperative Extension office, doing my best to keep my temper in check, I need answers. But when I ask horticulture team leader Carlos Gutierrez if he's ever going to tell me why I'm being asked to transfer to the one region I asked to avoid, he deflects.

Again.

"I need to make a few farm visits south of here." Removing his 4-H ball cap, he scratches his head through his crazy thatch of hair. "How 'bout we get some lunch on the way?"

My stomach grumbles in response, so when he tells me that we're headed to Greene County, I suggest the Lick Your Fork diner. I offer to drive since I know those back roads like the back of my hand and so that Gomer can join us.

"You've never had a problem bringing him along on the job?" Carlos asks while I clip my dog's harness to the seat. "He's a little scary looking."

I give the big lug a scratch behind the ears. "Never have. Gomer's what they call a career-change dog."

"Like, you got him when you changed careers?"

"Well, yeah, I adopted him right before I started working at CCE." I don't mention my previous employer. People at the extension tend to have strong opinions about Congento. "But it's the nice way of saying he's a service dog who flunked out."

"Was he a police dog?" Carlos twists in his seat to get a better look at Gomer. "Isn't that what German shepherds do?"

"He's actually a Belgian Malinois." I catch my dog's eye in the rearview. Just looking at him tends to calm me down when I'm anxious. "The breed is popular with law enforcement and the military, but Gomer was trained to be a seizure alert dog."

"So why'd he flunk out?"

"He failed the smell test."

Carlos leans toward Gomer and sniffs a few times. "Smells fine to me. But then again, I spend half my day tromping through manure."

"It's not about what *he* smells like. His nose isn't good enough. Part of his job was to detect the chemical changes in the human body when a seizure is coming on. He couldn't do it reliably."

"And they couldn't, like, retrain him for something else?"

"Funnily enough, he's also too friendly. That's a big no-no for assistance dogs."

"How'd you end up with him?"

"I just applied. Paid a pretty steep fee to help cover the cost of breeding and training him."

What I don't say? He's also turned out to be good for my mental health. Instead of sharing that news with the guy who may be my new boss, I give him the spiel I give farmers when they meet him for the first time. "He's kind of an icebreaker for me. He helps carry equipment, but because he was trained to find his owner's cell phone and medical bag, if I leave something behind in the truck, he'll find it and bring it to me—sometimes before I realize I've forgotten it. People think it's hilarious."

By the time we get to the diner, Carlos has warmed up to Gomer considerably. Sadly, that's not the case for Lick Your Fork's head waitress.

"Samuel Bedd." Latonya stops us with a hand in the air. "You cannot bring that dog in here."

"But he's a—"

"If you are about to tell me that this mutt is an"—she makes air quotes—"*emotional support animal* or what have you, you'd best be telling the truth. Because you know I'm gon' be on the phone to your grandmama before you say boo."

I consider blustering through, but then realize that I don't need to be on my grandmother's radar. Not until I figure out what the heck's going on with my job. "Fine. We'll take it to go."

Latonya tips her head to the side. "We have outside seating now, you know. In the back."

"Oh, okay." I raise my brows at Carlos, and he shrugs in response. "Can Gomer sit out there?"

Latonya gives Carlos a nice long look over. "If this is Gomer, he can sit wherever he pleases. Including my—"

"Latonya! Gomer is the dog." I gesture to my

colleague, who doesn't seem disturbed by Latonya's perusal. "*This* is Carlos."

Unrepentant, Latonya shoots him a feral smile. "The offer still stands. Nice to meet you, honey."

Squelching a shudder, I tap my thigh. Gomer comes to heel as we follow a gravel path around the diner.

"Seat yourselves," Latonya calls. "I'll be out there in a minute with menus. Two coffees?"

"Yes, ma'am," I yell back.

After we're settled, Carlos looks around the patio, set up with planters full of summer-blooming perennials and colorfully striped market umbrellas. Tapping the bright red composite decking making up our picnic table, he says, "Nice place. I don't know why I never stopped in before."

"Fork Lick's easy to miss."

"How do you know about it?"

"I grew up here."

"On a farm?"

I wince, not really wanting to get into it. "Uh, kind of."

"How do you 'kind of' grow up on a farm?"

Pulling a water bottle and portable dog bowl from my messenger bag, I give Carlos the Cliff's Notes of my tragic tale. "We lived in town, and my dad worked the family farm with my grandfather. But after my parents died, my siblings and I moved onto the farm proper."

"I'm sorry for your loss. How old were you, if you don't mind my asking?"

"I was twelve."

Thankfully, before Carlos delves further into family history, Latonya arrives to take our orders. Once we're alone again, Carlos clears his throat. "You know that having roots in a community makes you a more effective extension agent, right?"

Busying myself with stirring sugar into my coffee, I nod.

"Then why didn't you request an assignment in eastern New York in the first place?"

Before I can let out a frustrated groan, Gomer noses my hand, and I remember to take a deep breath before answering. "The problem with growing up here is that everybody—including my family—sees me as the nerdy kid who may have won all the science fairs, but also never buttoned his shirt right."

"Seems like you've got that problem figured out." Carlos' gaze tracks to my shirt front, and I run a hand up my chest to check the buttons, before I remember that I'm wearing a CCE polo.

Pushing my glasses back up my nose, I cough out a laugh as bitter as the coffee Latonya poured us. "Nobody around here's going to listen to my advice, not when my family's farm is failing."

"Every farm has its challenges. Especially small ones."

"How about seven hundred and fifty thousand dollars' worth of debt?"

Carlos blanches. "That is… a challenge."

"Even worse, they're growing soybeans. Monoculture. Stripping the soil and sinking cash into fertilizer and pesticides year after year."

"Did you suggest small grains or maybe hay as an alternative?"

"Yes, Carlos, I'm not an idiot," I snap. Gomer whines, and I blow out a breath. "I'm sorry. This gets me all kinds of riled up. I knew the farm was headed for trouble, even when I was in undergrad. But my grandfather wouldn't listen to me."

Carlos nods. "That's tough."

"Worse, now my older brother Ethan's equally resistant to change." I roll my eyes. "At least he was until his girl-friend blew back into town with her grand ideas. Now they're growing strawberries."

Before Carlos can say anything further, Latonya shows up with our sandwiches. We eat in silence until I can't take it anymore. "So do you see why it's a terrible idea for me to work here?"

Carlos wipes his mouth carefully and folds his hands on the table in front of him before meeting my gaze. "That isn't the only reason you're being considered for a move."

"What's that supposed to mean?"

"As you know, CCE likes to rotate new hires through a few different regions for the first year or so. But your supervisor out in Erie County had some frustrations with your work, and I was the only team leader interested in mentoring you."

"Are you serious?" Shame has my face heating. My hand instinctively finds Gomer, fingers sliding through his fur.

Carlos nods, his expression grave. "Your passion is appreciated, but your attitude is a problem. You can't goad people into doing things differently."

"Is this because of that sweet corn grower in Springville with Stewart's wilt?" I sit back, crossing my arms over my chest. "All I told him was the truth, and he got pissed off."

"Let me guess." Carlos mimics my posture. "You told

him we haven't yet developed varieties resistant to the disease."

"Exactly. Climate change is real. Things are changing fast. You have to adapt to survive." The farmer's angry face surfaces in my memory. "I told him about grant programs for solar farming as an alternative."

"We're talking about people's entire lives, son. Their family history. You must get it."

"Oh, I totally get stubbornness and refusal to try new things."

"In their minds, change is a risk."

"Not changing is a bigger risk."

"Traditions as old as these hills can't just be uprooted. A farmer coming to us for guidance is a great first step. We have to respect their experience."

"What do I do if they refuse to look forward? If they insist that this is the way we've always done things. This worked in the past. Well, buddy, research tells me that ain't gonna work anymore."

"Change takes money, effort and knowledge. We can provide the latter, and often some funding, but they've got to be ready, willing and able to put in the elbow grease. Which isn't always the case."

"What am I supposed to do differently, then?"

"Join my team. Tag along with me for the first couple weeks."

"So you can confirm that I'm a problem child?" I snap back.

"Is that what you think you are?"

Feeling like I'm repeating the same mistakes over and over in my life, I avoid answering his question. Instead, I take another bite of my sandwich, which now feels like sandpaper in my mouth. After I labor through chewing and swallowing, something occurs to me. "Do I actually have a choice in the matter?"

"You could be reassigned to the central office in Ithaca, but you wouldn't be working directly with farmers. You'd probably assist with research instead." Before I can ask more about that, Carlos leans forward, resting folded hands on the table. "Look. Roger told me you're the smartest he's got. I think we can learn from each other. Plus, I'm not getting any younger. My job'll be opening up in a few years. This district is your best shot for moving up."

Something's not right here. "If I'm so difficult, why would you even consider me to replace you?"

He snorts. "I'm too old to be intimidated by you, and I actually think we'd be a good team. You're up on all the latest and greatest, while I've got experience dealing with recalcitrant farmers."

"Want to meet my brother?"

He tips his head to the side, a shaggy eyebrow lifting. "Maybe he'll listen to me. Sometimes fresh eyes and ears are helpful."

I cough-laugh, coffee going up my nose.

Carlos hands me an extra napkin. "What's so funny?"

Wiping my mouth, I clear my throat. I don't think Carlos is as old as my grandmother, but the crow's-feet crinkling the terra-cotta skin surrounding his eyes are as deep as hers. "No offense, but... you're not exactly the epitome of fresh."

Carlos actually harrumphs. "I've still got game, son."

I don't want to know what that looks like, especially after the way he and Latonya were making eyes at each other. Thankfully, I'm saved by the bell or, rather, the Elton John song "Daniel" that my twin sister made her ringtone. I send her to voicemail, but if I don't text her, she'll worry. "Sorry, that's my sister," I explain to Carlos. "I'll just let her know I'm not dead."

> Me: Can't talk rn, whassup

> Colleen: Are you in town?

> Me:

> Colleen: I thought I felt a disturbance in the twin-verse.

My sister always texts full sentences, including punctuation, but she's fast. Before I can respond, she jumps down my digital throat.

> Colleen: What the heck, Sam? Were you even going to stop by?

"Everything okay?" Carlos asks. He sure is extra for an old guy.

"Yeah, she's just being nosy," I explain as I type out a reply.

> Me: I'm working

> Colleen: I thought you worked on the other side of the state.

Shit. Now I'm screwed.

> Me: I might be getting transferred

Colleen: To Fork Lick?

Me: Kinda

Colleen: Where are you staying?

Me: Not sure

Colleen: You better come home, Sam.
Gran's heart will be broken if she
finds out.

Wincing, I look up. Instead of checking his own phone like a normal person, Carlos is just waiting expectantly. "I'll never hear the end of it if my grandmother finds out I was within spitting distance of the farm and didn't stop by. Any chance we can slot in a stop after lunch?"

Carlos's smile is a little too pleased for my comfort. "It's a farm, ain't it? Visits are part of the job."

Maybe it'll be good for my new boss to see what I'm up against. I just hope neither of us regrets it.

CHAPTER 6
SAM

EVERY TIME I PULL UP IN FRONT OF MY GRANDPARENTS' farmhouse, a fresh wave of grief laced with guilt rolls over me. Gomer must feel it too, because the moment I turn off the engine, he squirms out of his harness and sets his jaw on my forearm, pressing heavily. After giving him a scratch behind the ears to let him know I'll be okay, I hop out of the truck and open the back door so he can hop out.

Gesturing for Carlos to follow, I head around the porch to the side door to use the boot scraper before ushering him and my dog into the kitchen. Something's simmering on the stove, so I know my grandmother must be around somewhere.

After yelling upstairs, I try the basement.

"Samuel? Is that you?" she calls from below. "I'll be right up."

But the moment she appears, she says, "Samuel, get that dog out of the kitchen."

"Gran, Gomer is trained to be with me at all times."

"You know I don't like animals in the house."

"I've seen your sheep in the living room."

"Only when there's a flood warning."

"Gomer's not a pet, Gran. He's a service animal."

"I think there's a reason why he failed at that, and you know it. He's not any smarter than his namesake."

"Namesake?"

"Gomer Pyle. From the TV show?"

"Never heard of it."

"I suppose it was on before you were born. In any case"—she marches to the screen door and opens it—"out, Gomer."

After a quick glance at me, he skulks past her to flop down on the porch with a grunt.

Gran pulls the door closed and then turns a sweet smile on Carlos. "Samuel, are you going to introduce your guest, or are you going to make this man think I didn't raise you right?"

"I'm Carlos, ma'am. Sam's new boss." Carlos offers both his hand and a smile that's a bit too flirtatious. "Lovely home you have here."

"Ethel Bedd," she says, shaking his hand. "So nice to meet you. What happened to his old boss?"

"I might be getting transferred," I say, unwilling to give in just yet, "to the Columbia and Greene Counties' office."

My grandmother's smile widens. "Well, that's wonderful. So you'll be staying here?"

"No, I, uh… It might not happen, and if it does, it won't be for several weeks."

"Well, you let me know if that changes." Her lips twist to the side. "I have two WWOOFers moving in later this month. I was going to put them in your old bedroom. But you could take the attic."

"Since when do we have WWOOFers?" Even though

my brother begrudgingly allowed me to hook him up with some Cornell Ag student interns over spring break, anytime I'd suggested the family bring in volunteer labor in exchange for room and board with a program like World Wide Opportunities on Organic Farms, my ideas had been shot down. Just like all my plans for the farm.

"When Lia started setting up the new community market, I expanded my kitchen garden and canning operation. I need help, and we have the room." She gestures vaguely upstairs. "So I signed up, and these girls are coming."

"I wish you'd've talked to me first," I said, struggling to keep my temper in check. "I could've gotten you set up with people who know what they're doing. But of course, no one ever listens to my ideas, whereas anything Lia or Molly says goes."

"We're doing just fine, Samuel—which you'd know if you ever came home." My grandmother would never raise her voice at me in front of a stranger, but her tone shifts just enough to cut.

"I'm sorry, Gran. I've just been—"

"Busy," she says, finishing for me. "I know you work hard. In any case, you are always welcome here."

"I know, Gran. But it makes more sense for me to have a place near the main office."

Her lips press together briefly, but she forces a smile as she turns to Carlos. "I'd feed you all lunch, but I promised I'd pick up Diane from the Crowders' farm."

"We ate at the diner. Just wanted to stop by and say hello," I say before the name registers. "Who is Diane?"

"Your sister's friend from college. She came to interview me about the seed saving last week, and she stayed to make videos with some of my friends."

A woman named Diane who's interested in seeds? Could it be the same person? She didn't say anything about doing interviews, but it's not like we got into too much detail about work.

"Where *is* Colleen?" I ask, wondering if I can find out more.

My grandmother waves a hand in the air. "She went into town for something. I can't remember what."

"Excuse me, Gran. I'm just going to let her know I stopped by." Stepping into the dining room, I mutter, "Since she's the one who told me to."

Me: I'm here. Where are you

Colleen: I had to do some errands.

Me: Do you have a photo of Diane

Me: The woman who is here interviewing people

Colleen: Why?

Me: Just curious

Colleen: Seriously?

Me: Do you have a picture or not

Colleen: Look at my Instagram. I posted a photo from a Vassar thing. It's the two of us standing on either side of a cutout tree a month ago.

After swiping over to the app, I scroll through my

sister's feed. A breath whooshes out of me when I find her. The woman I've dreamt about for months, the player I've missed battling on Trivia Crush, is here.

In Fork Lick?

If I weren't the one driving this afternoon, I could maybe figure out an excuse to stick around until Diane returns. But if I am going to work with Carlos, I can't skip out on him in the middle of the workday. Maybe it's for the best. She probably hates me. And if, by some miracle, she doesn't, I'd probably just screw things up anyway.

"It was great to meet you, Mrs. Bedd, but we've got to get to an appointment," Carlos is saying as he and my grandmother join me in the dining room.

Feeling like I've been caught doing something naughty, I shove my phone in my pocket.

"At least come to Sunday dinner when you get back in town, sweetheart." Her tone has softened, and my grandmother's warm hand grips my forearm as she gives me a brief peck on the cheek. "Even if you're not going to stay here. Your sister and brothers would love to see you."

"Um, I have to check my schedule, but I might be able to get back this weekend."

"Come if you can, honey. And you're welcome too, Carlos. Anytime."

"Thank you, ma'am. I might just take you up on that." He inhales deeply and tips his head toward the stove. "Something tells me you're a wonderful cook."

"I get by," Gran says, her cheeks pinking up. "Say hi to Baabara on your way out."

On the front porch, after I call Gomer, Carlos asks, "Is Barbra your sister?"

"Baabara is my grandmother's pet sheep," I say,

emphasizing the bleat in her name and pointing to the monstrosity of a shed as we pass it. "And *that* is her palace."

"Oh. Impressive." Hard to say if he's too shocked by the turreted sheep cote or what, but Carlos doesn't say anything else until we're back in the truck, where he just gives me the address of his first afternoon appointment. After I've punched it into my phone and we're on the way, he clears his throat. "You got a little testy with your grandmother there, son."

"I know," I admit, half my brain stuck on that photo of Diane. "It's just so frustrating. They never, ever listen to me. Not when my grandfather was alive, and not now."

"Hm. That does sound frustrating." He shuffles through his bag, pulls out a file folder, and studies its contents.

"So, what? You're not going to tell me what I should've done instead?"

"Do you want me to?"

"Isn't that the point? Of me"—I swoop a hand in the air between us—"coming to work with you?"

He closes the file and looks out the window, but I doubt he's really seeing the rolling hills lined with crops passing by. After an uncomfortably long silence, he says, "If you weren't talking to your family, would you have said things any differently?"

"I'd keep my tone more level, but I'd still make the same suggestions—the ones I've brought up time and time again. Consider diversifying. Hops would be an excellent choice, especially with the grant support that's on offer and the new laws limiting New York brewers to working with state-grown crops. But what do they do? Plant strawberries because my brother's girlfriend—who is a banker, not a soil scientist—thinks it's a good idea."

"It sounds like you may have skipped an important first step."

"I tested the soil and water a long time ago. I know that—"

"Not that step," he says. "Did you ever ask your family about their goals for the farm?"

"Not in so many words. But it's my farm too."

"Are you the one putting in the work?"

"Not exactly, but it's obvious what they—*we*—should do. It's basic stuff… if the goal is to hang onto the farm, that is."

Carlos nods as I continue to vent my frustrations with the choices my grandfather and now Ethan have made for the farm, as well as the many suggestions I've made for changes, all of which have been ignored. When I finally run out of steam, he's silent for so long I wonder if I'm going to get fired or something. Finally, he clears his throat. "I can tell you're a quick thinker. I imagine that your brain cycles through all the potential solutions to a problem, perhaps faster than you're aware of. But as an outsider, you can never know all the variables. Even on your own family farm, if you're not there on a day-to-day basis."

"Sure, but I still—"

Carlos holds up a hand to stop me before I can get going again. "I'm going to suggest that you make an effort to slow your own brain down. Ask what the client's goals are. Listen before you speak. Take it all in. Go back to the office, come up with all the ways we can help them meet their goals, then present those to the client so they see all the possibilities and what investments they'll have to make. Then, you let them come to their own conclusions."

He pauses, and when I glance over, he raises his hands in the air and then lets them drop onto his thighs with a slap. "It's the only way I know how to get buy-in."

He lets me sit with this speech until we've pulled into the driveway of the farm we're visiting and I've turned off the engine. Then he holds out a folder labeled with the farm's name in block print. "If you like, you can start here."

I open the folder, but the words swim on the page. I can't seem to get past wanting to see Diane again. I mean, she might not even remember me. She probably won't want to talk to me. But I still want to try. I never got a second chance with my grandfather. I'm not going to waste this one.

"Sounds like a plan," I say to Carlos, closing the folder. But before I join him outside the truck, I tap out a text to my sister.

> Me: Tell Gran I'll be at Sunday dinner

> Colleen: Yay! And I really hope you're moving back. I miss you.

> Me: Miss you too, Ree.

Dealing with my family at Sunday dinner is worth it if it means a chance to win over my ice-loving trivia queen.

Unfortunately, that's not what the universe had in mind for me, because instead of staying in the Hudson Valley for the weekend, I get a call from my landlord that has me racing back to the place I've called home for the past six months: my apartment near the CCE Erie County offices. Instead of spending the weekend trying to woo Diane, I end up dealing with the aftermath of a burst water pipe in my ceiling.

Good news is I won't have to break my lease to take the transfer. Bad news—or more good news depending on how you look at it—all the fancy suits I bought on Congento's dime are toast. Along with most of my furniture and half my books.

Also, I completely forget about Sunday dinner until I wake up Monday morning to a string of texts from my sister.

Colleen: Sam, where are you?

Colleen: Are you coming to dinner or not?

Colleen: This is not good.

Colleen: Dammit, Sam. Call me. You'd better have a good reason for missing this.

Colleen: Are you dead? You'd better not be dead.

Groaning, I type out an apology.

Me: Sorry, sorry. I had to go back to Buffalo

Colleen: I thought you were coming to Sunday dinner.

Me: My apartment flooded

Me: Most of my stuff is ruined

Colleen: So are your chances with Diane.

Me: What are you talking about

Colleen: Did you or did you not have a
thing with her?

Me: How do you know about that

Colleen: So the answer is yes!

Elton John starts up, and I realize I left my sister hanging. I don't want to face the twin interrogation, but I do want to know what she meant about me losing my chance with Diane.

She starts talking the moment I accept the call. "The dinner you missed? It was one for the record books."

"What do you mean?"

"Ethan and Alex got into a huge fight."

"They were both there?" From what I've gathered, Alex hasn't shown up for Sunday dinner—an important tradition for our grandmother—for years. Not that I have either, but at least I, like our youngest brother Jackson, have the excuse of living and working elsewhere. Alex lives just down the road.

"It was a total shitshow, Sam-Dan."

When my kindergarten-teaching sister curses *and* uses my childhood nickname, I know things are bad. I no longer have a couch, so I lean on the kitchen counter as Gomer presses against my leg. "What happened?"

She groans. "Everything our brothers have been mad

about for the past ten years got dredged up. Right in front of Diane. She made some excuses and left before anyone got up this morning. Gran's really upset."

Before I can ask if they know where she went, my sister adds, "You should've been here, Sam."

I cough out a laugh. "Believe me, if I'd been there, it would've been worse."

There's a long silence, and I pull my phone from my ear, thinking that the call got dropped. It's still live, so I put it on speaker. "You still there?"

"Sam-Dan, why do you hate us so much?"

Suddenly so tired I can barely hold up my head, I set my phone on the counter, take off my glasses, and slump onto my forearms. I used to tell my sister everything. Everything G-rated, anyway. But ever since I quit Congento and fought with my grandfather, I haven't been able to.

"Sam?"

"I'm here."

"I really do miss you, Sam-Dan."

"I know. Me too."

And then it becomes clear. It's bad enough that Grandad died hating me. I don't want the rest of my family thinking that I hate them. It's probably a good thing that Diane left again, though, because mending my family's fences is not going to be pretty.

"I have to finish out my assignment here, Colleen. But then I'm coming home."

CHAPTER 7
SAM

HAVING SAID GOODBYE TO MY COLLEAGUES IN THE CCE ERIE County offices, I arrive for Sunday dinner only a month later than I'd planned, with what's left of my belongings in bags and boxes in the back of my truck. After I put Gomer in a sit-stay on the porch, I squat in front of him and run my hands over his soft fur. "Wish you could come inside and keep me calm, buddy. But I'm trying to play by the rules."

After all that, I'm a little disappointed when the only person I find inside is Ethan's new/old girlfriend Lia. At least when she looks up from chopping vegetables, she smiles at me.

"Gran put you to work?" I ask.

"She's downstairs picking herbs for the chicken salad."

Lia's cheeks are a nice rosy pink. She's looking a heck of a lot healthier than she did when she showed up at the reading of my grandfather's will last winter. I'm trying to figure out if it's rude to comment on that, when she hands me a bunch of carrots. "So you're back in town now too?"

As I scrub and peel them, we fill each other in on the job changes that brought each of us back to Fork Lick.

"Sounds like you really love what you're doing these days," she says.

"It's super rewarding. I'm only making a fraction of what I did at Congento, but who needs money?"

Her smile is strained as she trades the carrots for celery, and as I rinse the stalks, I remember who needs money: my brother Ethan and our family farm.

"This is kind of awkward," I begin, "because you work for the bank and all, but you're a friend too, so…"

When I trail off, she places a hand on my forearm and squeezes it lightly. "You can trust me, Sam. Your family is important to me."

I blow out a breath. "I've just wondered, were the loans Grandad took out legit? I mean, was the lender predatory in any way?"

She tips her head to the side and looks out the window over the sink—not like she's focusing on the crop rows fanning out over the land that's been in our family for more than a century, but like she's looking at spreadsheets in her head. "I really don't think so. The timing doesn't line up with that era. All the loans were approved for equipment purchases and other farm expenses. I'm sure each refinance made sense at the time. Your grandfather just had a streak of bad luck."

We're quiet for a few minutes, back to slicing and dicing, but when she sniffs, I ask, "You okay?"

"Just, you know, onions." She waves a hand in front of her face. "But I did remember one thing that was a little unusual. One year, he took out a loan with a line item marked 'Personal.' I think it was about fifty grand. I haven't been able to figure out what it was for."

A chill runs down my spine, and I fumble the potatoes. Turning off the water, I take a deep breath. "Do you remember when that was?"

"Pretty sure it was six years ago. Does that amount or time frame ring a bell?"

"No, not really," I lie, swallowing down the urge to confess the truth. "Probably, you know, none of my business."

If only that were the case.

Grandad may have made some bad decisions; he may have treated me like I was a pain in the ass and more trouble than he'd planned on in this lifetime. But it sounds like he also dug himself deeper into debt to put me through school.

And then it all comes back—his words shouted in anger the Saturday after Thanksgiving last year, right after I quit my job and found a new one I could be proud of.

Right before he died.

"You're the smartest kid in this family, but you have no sense. Why'd you have to leave Congento?"

"Because it felt like selling my soul to the devil, Grandad. I hated it there."

"Your family made sacrifices to put you through the best school in the country."

"And I'm using that education. The Cooperative Extension helps small family farms. Like this one."

"Help? All you ever do is propose outlandish ideas that cost money I don't have. Not sure how that's helpful."

"If you weren't so damn stubborn, you'd see that change is

inevitable. And if you paid attention, you'd have known that Congento was killing me."

All I want right now is to be comforted. To run to my grandmother, the way I did when I got bullied as a middle-schooler, and ask her if Grandad hated me.

But she has her own grief to deal with.

I need to figure out a way to erase that debt. And I need to present those ideas in a way that doesn't set my brother's hair on fire. I can't make the same mistake with Ethan that I made with my grandfather.

I don't know what I was thinking, imagining a future with Diane. I can't even manage a relationship with my own family. Luckily for her, she got out before I had a chance to try.

CHAPTER 8
DIANE

EVEN THOUGH IT WAS UNCOMFORTABLE AS HELL TO SIT through, I was impressed at the family dinner last month when Colleen's brothers got it all out on the table, so to speak. So unlike my stiff upper lip family, where you'd never know what anyone is feeling. If they're feeling anything. Sometimes, I'm not sure.

Still, it took some convincing for Ethel to get me to return to Fork Lick. It's not like I was planning to stay forever, but it was clear she was disappointed when I left so abruptly. I get the feeling she didn't stand up for herself before she was widowed, but for the past few weeks, Ethel Bedd didn't let up with the phone messages and texts until I agreed to return.

I'll admit that the videos I posted after my visit here seem to have hit a chord. Every single one I put up is getting hundreds of thousands of likes and comments, even without a shirtless farmer.

Well... there was that one shot I got at the dairy of *two* shirtless farmers, Alex and one of his guys, tossing bales down from the hay loft. And I may have put it in slo-mo, but that's because it was the only way the viewer could see the way wisps of hay and dust caught the light.

Every other video focused on seeds, whether it was interviews with the other members of Ethel's co-op or drone shots of row upon row of heirloom varieties thriving in this upstate New York microclimate, nestled between the Catskills and the Hudson River. I even got the time lapse feature to work for once and made a cool video of a row of bright green sprouts emerging from dark brown soil.

It smelled like cow poop, but my viewers will never have to know.

Anyway, Ethel assures me that Ethan and Alex have made up and that tonight's Sunday dinner will be a peaceful one. The minute we wrap a quick shoot where Ethel demonstrates the best ways to harvest herbs, we'll be heading upstairs where said herbs will get mixed in with heirloom green beans, cherry tomatoes, boiled potatoes, and a neighbor's chicken to make a hearty salad that already has my mouth watering. Even better, dessert is a berry crumble topped with ice cream made from Udderly Creamy milk–Ethel is helping them expand their product offerings, and we're testing out cheeses and milks.

"I think I've got what I need," I tell her, checking the footage briefly on my camera.

"As do I," Ethel says, holding up a metal bowl piled with fragrant herbs.

Promising her that I'll be in shortly to help out in the kitchen, I take the steps from the basement that lead directly outside to stow equipment in my car. The first time I stayed here, Ethel had ordered me to enter the house through the side door without knocking, "like family."

The phrase warmed my heart and sliced it open in equal measure. If only I were a member of this family. Or any family that wasn't my own.

I've learned my lesson, though. Best not to get too close to my subjects. This time, I found a VRBO to rent while I interview the rest of the folks in Fork Lick and, as she has requested, give Ethel pointers on shooting her own videos.

The sun has dipped behind the hills, meaning dark's falling quickly as I lock my Subaru. My belly grumbles as I take the porch steps, making me wonder if I'm good enough at shooting food to add cooking and recipes to my video lineup. People need inspiration to grow their own food, right? Need to know what to do with it? As I round the corner of the house, a scrabbling sound yanks me out of my head seconds before a furry beast barrels into me.

I let out a super embarrassing girly squeal before I register that it's just a very friendly, very large dog. German shepherd, maybe. Whatever he is, he seems very excited to see me because he can't stop wiggling. Stroking over his soft fur, I try to calm him down.

"Who are you, buddy?" I ask, but that just makes him whine and wiggle more. Before I know it, I'm on my ass and he's licking my face.

I'm trying to figure out if the dog has a collar and tag, when a man barks, "Gomer! Off!"

There's something about that voice, something that sends a shiver of excitement down my spine, but I can't quite—

"Oh my god," he says. I've heard those exact words gritted out in passion in that voice. Just the thought of it has my nipples perking up and aiming themselves in his direction.

Words pour out of his mouth as he pulls the dog off me —apologies, reassurance that he's friendly, that he never acts like this—but I'm too stunned to react.

Happy memories of the night I spent with this man vie with enraged ones from the following morning when I learned what kind of person he really is. Not to mention the way his testimony ramped up my own residual guilt.

Now, I'm mostly confused at what I see in the dim light. There isn't a suit in sight. The knees of his Carhartt work pants are streaked with mud. A faded t-shirt strains across a chest that's more defined than I remember. Rolled up sleeves reveal corded forearms, now tanned instead of pale. His hair is longer too, curling at his collar and flopping over his brow, more Henry Cavill in *Night Hunter* than *Superman*.

But the ice blue eyes and full lower lips are the same.

"My grandmother made me tie him up out here," he says. "So he's probably extra squirmy. But he wouldn't intentionally hurt a fly."

"Ethel is your grandmother?"

Hope surges behind my breastbone. Colleen's a twin, so maybe this guy's a twin too—the twin of the asshole who testified before the state assembly, not the man himself.

"Are you okay, Diane? Did he hurt you?"

"I don't think so," I say, even as I check my arms and legs for scrapes. I don't feel hurt, but I'm kind of having an out-of-body experience right now. But wait, if this is the *good* twin… "Hang on. How do you know my name?"

"Are you sure you didn't hit your head?" Squinting, he steps closer. "Do you not remember me? Samuel? Daniel12051 on Trivia Crush?"

When he reaches down to help me up, I scoot out of reach. "So you're not a twin?"

His brow furrows. "No. I am. A twin."

"An identical twin?" I ask hopefully.

He shakes his head slowly. "I'm a fraternal twin. Colleen's twin."

"Not a twin of one of her brothers?"

He side-eyes me like he's now sure I hit my head. "My brothers don't have twins."

Disappointment lands on my chest with a crushing blow. "So you're Samuel."

"That's what I said. We met in Albany. Just nine months ago."

The dog squeezes between us like he's protecting Sam. From me.

Want-to-kiss-him hormones flood my body, but anger throws up a dam. If he's the evil twin, I'm mad at him. Scrabbling to my feet, I straighten my spine and pin back my shoulders. He may be a head taller than me, but that doesn't mean I can't face him down. "Not that it's any of your business, but I'm invited to dinner. If you'll excuse me, I need to wash up and help with the preparations."

"Wait," he says, grabbing my elbow.

When I look down at his hand pointedly, he frees me. "Sorry, I just… uh…"

I meet his gaze, brows raised in challenge.

"Maybe at dinner we can pretend we don't know each other?" he asks.

My cheeks heat with shame, but I lift my chin, banishing it. He's the one who should be embarrassed. "Fine with me. We don't ever need to speak again. Besides things like, you know, pass the salt."

"That's not what I—"

Hand in the air between us, I stop his words. "You don't need to explain."

And then I hustle inside.

I need to wash my hands after the encounter with the dog, but I also need a minute to catch my breath, so I slip through the screen door into the kitchen, past the pre-dinner chaos, and duck into the hall bathroom. There, I scrub my hands, wishing I could scrub my brain—and maybe even my vagina—splash water on my face and tell my girl parts to calm the heck down.

This is not a chance for a do-over, I tell myself firmly. That man just happens to be a member of the family I wish were mine. But his employer is evil incarnate and goes against everything I believe in and work for.

I enter the kitchen with an expression of surprise pre-applied to my face in preparation for pretending to meet Sam, but it's quickly replaced by genuine astonishment. Instead of a warm welcome, everyone treats Sam like he's the stranger, not me. Colleen punches him with what could be construed as affection, but his brothers frown at him while Ethel points a wooden spoon at each of the siblings in turn. "No fighting at the table, boys, physical or otherwise. We have guests."

After they all mumble various versions of *Yes ma'am*, Ethel uses the spoon to point out the two WWOOFers she's brought on since I was last here, introducing them all around. Jane, a freckle-faced blonde, and Hetty, a brunette with a warm, tawny complexion, each lift a pint of beer in salutation. Ethel pokes Colleen with the spoon. "Are you going to introduce your friend to your brother?"

"Oh, right. Sorry, Diane." An odd expression passes over Colleen's face before she grabs Sam's elbow and drags him around the kitchen island. "Diane, this is Sam. Sam, this is Diane."

Ethel hoots. "Just like on *Cheers*!"

"You mean like on *New Girl*?" Jane asks.

"I never got past season one of that show," Ethel says. "But on *Cheers*, Sam and Diane were the kind of couple that hated each other—total opposites—but you rooted for them anyway."

"Huh," Hetty says. "On *New Girl*, you didn't really root for them as a couple. But they did end up together, I think."

"Didn't Diane end up moving to Paris to be a writer?" an unfamiliar male voice asks. "On *Cheers*?"

Sam's head whips around. "Wait. You're here too?"

"Too?" Ethan asks. "What do you mean *too*?"

"Uh… I-I don't know," Sam mumbles. "I just… I'm surprised Sunday dinner is so crowded all of a sudden."

"To answer your question, your grandmother invited me. Remember?" The stranger waves at me from a spot in the corner. "I'm Carlos, Diane. Sam's boss."

Whaaat? This guy is not at all what I'd expect from a Congento executive. I mean, it's the weekend, so I know he wouldn't be in a three-piece suit. But a handlebar mustache? Shaggy salt-and-pepper hair that'd rival Einstein's? A flannel shirt that's seen better days?

Doesn't seem like a C-suite type. At least not the ones I know.

A kitchen timer dings, biscuits are whisked from the oven, and then the whirl of activity is back until we're all settled at the table for dinner. Sam manages to find a seat diagonally across and at the other end of the table from me, which suits me just fine. I don't have to talk to him, but I can study him without being obvious.

Why does he have to be so damned attractive? He's as sexy in dirt-covered work attire as he was in a perfectly pressed dress shirt. As scrumptious as he was naked.

Le sigh. I think naked might be my favorite.

"I hear you've got a YouTube channel focusing on seed preservation," Carlos says, breaking into my estrogen-laced thoughts.

After fumbling my fork until it hits my plate with a clatter, I manage to catch it before it hits the floor.

"You okay there?" Sam asks.

"Fine. Just, you know, clumsy." I hold up the fork like it's a prize before spearing a chunk of chicken salad and stuffing it into my mouth.

This doesn't deter Carlos, who just waits patiently.

Once I've chewed a long time, swallowed, and washed it down with water, I nod. "That's right."

"I'd love to hear more about it." He butters his biscuit all casual, like he's not pumping me for intel so he and his big guns at The Seed Alliance can try and take me down.

I shake my head. "I doubt you'd find it interesting."

"She's very talented," Ethel says. "I couldn't believe what all she did with my interview. Added all kinds of music and little cartoons and everything. Made me out like a superhero."

"You and your club are heroes, Ethel," I say, my passion for the subject overriding my well-founded wariness around the Congento boys. "In the United States alone, we've lost ninety percent of our fruit and vegetable varieties. You're an essential part of the effort to protect what little crop diversity remains."

Carlos, seemingly oblivious to the not-so-subtle digs I'm making at his company's expense, continues to ask questions until I can't take it anymore.

"What, total vertical integration isn't enough for you? You've got to stamp out every tiny little effort to undermine Congento's ever-growing control of our food supply?"

His brow wrinkles, and he tips his head to the side. "Congento?"

I point my fork at him and then at Sam. "Aren't you his boss? At Congento?"

Sam clears his throat and then raises his brow to speak slowly. "I don't work there anymore. I quit nine months ago."

Wait. Sam and I met nine months ago.

"You quit? Nine months ago?" The phrase echoing in my head as well as my mouth, gravity wins, and my fork hits the floor.

"How did you know Sam worked at Congento?" Colleen asks, like she's acting out a part.

I blow out a breath. "Because the last time I saw him, he did."

Sam wipes his mouth with his napkin, folds it, and places it next to his plate. "May Diane and I be excused, Gran?"

"But—" I begin. I mean, I'm all for a chance to yell at him and then jump his bones, and I don't want to do either in polite company, but I don't want to miss that berry dessert.

"We just need to discuss an important matter," Sam says, eyes on me. "We'll be back shortly."

Ethel narrows her eyes at Sam, while Colleen looks like she's about to burst out laughing. Feeling exposed, I get to my feet. "Yep. We'll be right back. Excuse me."

Without waiting for Sam, I make a beeline for the front door. Outside, I take a deep breath and keep walking, past the shed I know now truly is the sheep's home. So weird. I've almost made it to the pole barn by the time Sam catches me.

"That day at the state house," he growls, getting in my way. "You didn't give me a chance to explain."

"Explain why you lied to me? Or why you humiliated me?"

"It was my job."

"You could've at least given me a heads up."

"First off, I didn't know you'd be there." I step back, doing my best to hang onto my mad. He follows, his expression driving me back and making me want to rub up against him all at the same time. "Second, I didn't know that you work for a seed bank. Third, I had no idea that I was going to be on that panel. My boss was supposed to do it, but he got food poisoning."

"Lucky him. He didn't have to spout lies in front of a government commission. I mean, seriously? Agroterrorism?"

"I quit before I'd even left the building, Diane. I tried to find you, but you disappeared." His head tips to the side, and he narrows his eyes. "And now you're here getting all cozy with my family."

I throw a hand up between us. "I had no idea it was your family. And it doesn't look like you're terribly cozy with them, anyway."

"Yeah, well, that's a long story."

I blow out a breath. Oh, families and long stories we don't want to tell. But instead of admitting that, I double down. "You have no idea what you have here, you dummy."

He stiffens. "I may be a lot of things, but dumb is not one of them."

"Oh, yeah? Well you may be smart up here"—I reach up to knock once on his forehead, then tap his chest as I say—"but here? Not so much."

Suddenly, I'm pressed up against the pole barn. "What about here?" he asks, as he whispers a kiss below my ear.

Without checking with my brain, my hands grab the sides of his face and pull his mouth to mine. "About as smart as you are here," I snap, before covering it with my own.

And then it's on. He grabs my ass, hikes me up so we're level, and presses me up against the side of the barn. I never knew I had this fantasy, but I'm into it. My legs grip his slim waist, and my ankles lock behind his back as we devour each other.

Turns out, berry cobbler has nothing on this man and his mouth.

Or his hands. Which I need to feel on my bare skin. But just as I manage to untuck my shirt, something cold and wet hits my side, making me yelp. "What the—"

"Gomer, off!" Sam yells, stepping away so fast that I

almost land on my ass. The dog backs off too, but he doesn't go far, whining as his gaze flicks from me to his owner and back again.

"He's right, Sam. This is..." I push past him. "A bad idea."

And then I hightail it back to the house before I can get any other bad ideas.

CHAPTER 9
SAM

FOR THE THIRD TIME IN OUR SHORT ACQUAINTANCE DIANE disappears, leaving me dazed. I'm so discombobulated, in fact, that I'm not even sure what happened. Did I get to explain what happened the morning we testified? Did I apologize? Did my dog just cockblock me?

"Woof." Gomer noses around in the dirt before pressing something into my hands. It feels like a piece of fabric. I can't make out any details in the dim light, but when I bring it to my nose, a memory hits me: A curtain of brown hair tickling my chest and belly as Diane kisses her way down my torso.

Aaand I'm as desperate for her as I was five minutes ago.

She was wearing some kind of headband at dinner. It must've gotten knocked off when we were making out. "Thanks, buddy. If you had to get between us, at least now I have a reason to talk to her again."

But when I mount the steps to my grandmother's house, a different female is sitting alone on the porch swing.

"You okay Ree?" I ask my twin. When I was little, I couldn't make the "L" sound for a long time. At first I called her Kah-reen, but it eventually got shortened to Ree. She, on the other hand, articulated both my first and middle names perfectly and, like our mother, would call me Samuel Daniel whenever she was pissed at me, which eventually got shortened to Sam-Dan.

Better than my grandfather's nickname for me: Mule. As in the back end of Sam-muel.

She startles, like she was lost in thought. "Yeah, well, not exactly."

"Why didn't you tell me Diane was back?"

She smirks. "What would be the fun in that?"

Shoving the hairband in my pocket, I sigh. "Seriously?"

Gomer shoves his head under her hand, and she pets him absently. "Nah. I didn't know she was here until dinner. I guess Gran nagged her till she came back. Something about making videos about Baabara."

I settle next to her, careful to avoid jostling the dog. "I'm an idiot. When I saw her here on the porch before dinner, I panicked and asked her to pretend that we didn't know each other. But I think it made her mad."

"Kinda don't blame her, Sam."

"Like I said…"

"Yeah, yeah, you're an idiot. You're a man; what do you expect?"

Before I can ask her where her acid tone's coming from, she asks, "So when did you meet her?"

"Actually, we were Trivia Crush buddies for months last year, but then I met her in Albany." Skipping the overnight extracurricular activities, I add, "We were on opposite sides testifying before the state reps about seed banks."

"Didn't you quit right after that?"

"Yeah, but she didn't know that. She hates me, obviously."

"Not sure that's what's obvious."

I should probably ask for sisterly advice, but I'd rather talk about whatever's up with her. "So why are you sitting out here on the porch all moody and stuff?"

"I'm not—" She breaks off with a sigh, takes a breath like she's going to start again, then blows it out. She shakes her head briefly and then finally asks, "Do you, uh, think something's off with Jane?"

"Jane? Who's that?"

"The blond WWOOFer?"

I close my eyes, trying to remember anything about either of the women from dinner, but I was so thrown by Diane's presence I can't even picture her. "Sorry, I got nothing. You think there's something sketchy about her?"

Colleen grimaces. "Maybe? I'm not sure I trust my instincts these days."

"What do you mean?"

She shakes her shoulders, almost like she's shaking something off. "Nothing. Just… keep an eye on her, okay?"

I nod, sure that something's up with my sister, but I know better than to press. She'll tell me when she's ready. She always does. "Hey, I've been meaning to ask you something. Do you think you could suggest that Ethan call FarmNet?"

"What's FarmNet?"

"It's this nonprofit that's all about helping farmers with

their finances. I know Lia's done a lot, but if we still need to restructure or find some grants, it's a great resource."

"Why don't you do it?"

"Why do you think? He won't listen to me."

"Because of your high and mighty attitude."

"Fine, fine, I get it." I jump off the swing, flinging a hand in the air. "No need to hit me over the head with it."

She groans and steadies the swing with her foot. "What the hell, Sam?"

I groan too, but in frustration. "I'm sorry, I'm just— listen. Don't tell anybody else, but the reason I got transferred is that I'm apparently too *high and mighty* with our clients."

She wrinkles her nose. "Oh. Sorry to have hit that nerve right on the head. It's good to have you closer, though. We'll get to see you more."

"Yeah."

"Wow. Don't bowl me over with your excitement or anything."

"It's like I said," I say, my voice admittedly whiny. "No one listens to me."

"Maybe you could use us as practice. Try out new ways of speaking to clients with your family."

I scrub a hand through my hair. "Funny, that's what Carlos said. But I still think the FarmNet thing should come from you. It's too important to risk a blowup between Ethan and me. Anyway, didn't you say you wanted to come up with a business plan? That's what they're all about. Plus, they have resources."

She frowns at me for a moment, studying me, and I suddenly feel sorry for any kid in her class that misbehaves. "Okay, I'll do it. But only because I want to learn more too. Not because I'm letting you off the hook."

Getting up, she hooks an arm through mine and tugs me toward the door. "It's the Bedd Fellows Farm, you know. It's not Ethan's farm."

I think about what Carlos said, about the people who are here doing the work, but instead of copping to that, I say, "Maybe to you. The favorite."

"I'm not the favorite."

"Well, it sure as hell isn't me. I'm the ignored middle child."

"There is no middle if we're twins, dummy."

"Five minutes. I got five minutes on you, Ree."

"And a couple pounds," she adds, reminding me that, yet again, I'm the sibling who takes more than his share.

"Whatever." I open the door for her and gesture for her to precede me. "I'm the middle. Anyway, you're a girl."

"Gee, thanks, I hadn't noticed," she says, her tone bitter.

Yep, something's up with my twin.

"It makes you special," I say, backpedaling. Fighting with my brothers is status quo, but I can't take tension between the two of us. "Whereas I'm just another mouth to feed."

She turns, and I have to stop quickly to avoid crashing into her. "The poor-me thing doesn't look good on you, Sam-Dan. Might want to keep that in mind when you try to patch things up with Diane."

"What? What makes you think—"

But she stomps up the stairs and slams the door to her room before I can finish my sentence.

CHAPTER 10
DIANE

I HAVE GOT TO STOP HIDING IN THE BATHROOM. IT'S SILLY. Just because I kissed Sam does not make me weak. Thanks to the dog, I walked away before I could do anything stupid, like have sex up against the side of the barn.

By the time I got back to the house, dinner was over and everyone was in the kitchen cleaning up. Instead of helping, I booked it for the powder room, where I've been sitting for the past ten minutes.

I should probably just move on. There are plenty of other farmers and gardeners out there. But I feel like I've just scratched the surface here in Fork Lick. For a tiny hamlet—its official designation—it's packed full of people with good stories. Plus, I've gotten attached to this family.

But maybe that's the thing. I should leave before I get too attached. If they find out about my family, they'll probably hate me.

Footsteps sound in the hallway, so I run water in the sink so whoever is out there doesn't think I'm the kind of person who doesn't wash their hands after fake going to the bathroom. After I fake dry, however, I freeze, my hand halfway to the doorknob.

"Gran, she's basically a stranger," Sam says from right outside the door.

I should just step out so they'll stop talking about me, but I can't move.

"I think I'm a pretty good judge of character," Ethel snaps back.

"There are all kinds of predatory hucksters out there who specialize in stealing from the elderly."

He thinks I'm going to *steal* from Ethel? WTF!

"Are you saying I'm elderly, Samuel Daniel Bedd?"

"Well—"

"Because I bet I can beat you in Wordle. I do it every morning."

"I am sure you could. But you are recently widowed, which anyone can find out with a simple Google search."

If Ethel says anything in response, I can't hear it.

"Just promise me you won't give her any important information, okay, Gran? Please? I'm just trying to look out for you."

"Fine," she says on a huff. "But like I told you, she only…"

They must have started walking down the hall, because Ethel's voice fades to the point that I can't hear the end of the sentence. Instead of finally leaving the bathroom, I slump down onto the toilet.

I shouldn't feel so disappointed. After all, I know who Sam is: a soulless shark in a suit. Every time I start to think I misjudged him, he bares his teeth.

I promised Ethel I'd stick around for a week, and I'll do that. I can avoid Sam. It's not like he lives here, and I'm staying elsewhere too. Which reminds me—I still need the check-in info for my rental. But when I open the app and look for my reservation, it's not there. Searching my email, I find the original confirmation. Scrolling through it, I find a number for the host, but when I call it, the number's been disconnected.

"What the heck?"

"Are you okay in there, dear?"

"Gah!?" Startled at the sound of Ethel's voice, I leap to my feet, my phone flying out of my hands and into the sink. "Dang it."

"Diane?"

"I'm fine," I call through the door.

Shoving my phone in my back pocket, I wash my hands again, even though I never did actually use the toilet. Unfortunately, when I emerge from the powder room, Ethel's waiting with a concerned look on her face.

"I'm really fine, I promise." I wave towards the bathroom behind me. "Just, you know, got distracted on my phone."

She pats my arm. "Come into the parlor with me, honey."

"I really should get going," I begin, but then I remember that I no longer have a place to go *to*, so I follow her through a door across the hall. She turns on a lamp, which makes the little room even cozier, before settling onto the couch and patting the cushion next to her. Like the cat we had growing up that was never quite comfortable with humans, but still wanted to be close by, I perch on the edge of the cushion the farthest away from her.

Ethel picks up a bag, puts on her readers, and begins to knit. I'm curious about Samuel's childhood but asking seems like a bad idea. Especially since I've decided to avoid him. Noticing the framed photos that cover one wall, I hop up to get a closer look.

"Those go back over a hundred years," Ethel says. "My husband's family has lived on this land for a long time."

"It's so nice that it's been passed down from generation to generation." Pain pricks at my heart, the way it does every time I think about my family's orchard, which I'm pretty sure my mother sold from her phone on the way home from my grandmother's funeral. "It doesn't always work out that way."

She sniffs, but when I look over, her focus is on the wool and needles in her hands, so I can't quite read her expression. "That hasn't exactly been the case. About fifteen years ago now, Eugene was on the road to retirement. Our son and daughter-in-law were planning to take over. But when they were taken from us, Eugene had to work the farm all by himself until the boys got old enough to help, and we had five extra mouths to feed."

"That must've been hard," I say softly.

Ethel's hands idle, her gaze fixed on a photo next to me.

"That picture right next to you? That's Jim and Sandy with all five of their children a couple years before the accident. They were such good parents."

I find Samuel right away, even though he can't be more than ten years old. He and Colleen are right next to each other, like they're joined at the hip.

"Those poor babies," Ethel says, her voice thick with emotion. "Their parents passed away when they were only half-grown. Their grandfather and I did our best to finish the job, but I don't think we quite measured up."

"You've had a lot of loss."

She nods once, but her expression remains stoic. "We have. I still can't believe I'm a widow, and I miss my son and his wife every day, but I loved raising my grandkids. And I'm so proud of each and every one of them. Still, it's been nice to have a full house again. In fact, you know you're welcome to stay here again, as long as you need to. We have room. Jane and Hetty are sharing the attic."

As she says this, something clicks. Maybe that's what Sam was concerned about. Maybe he thinks I lied to his grandmother about needing a place to stay. The last thing I want is to take advantage of her generosity. I'm not going to confess everything about my situation, but I need to make sure she knows I'm not destitute or anything.

Sitting next to her, I say, "Ethel, when I said I was living out of my car, did you think I was homeless? Because I'm not."

Ethel pats my hand. "There's no shame in homelessness, dear. Though I think they call it unhoused these days. Or is it home free? No, that sounds like something else. I'm learning so much on the YouTube and the TikTok, but there's always more to keep up with."

Since she didn't really answer my question, I press further. "I just want to be clear. I can afford to rent an apartment. It just seemed wasteful to keep one up when I'm on the road all the time."

She tips her head to the side and studies me for a moment. "That may be true, but you do seem to need a home. And I've got one to share."

After getting up and looking out in the hall, she closes the door and returns to the sofa. "I'll tell you a secret. I was quite lonely this winter. Colleen was kind enough to move in with me after my husband died, but she has her own life to lead, as she should. Meanwhile, Ethan and Alex weren't speaking to each other, and Sam and Jackson were gone. I don't know if I'll ever have all my kids home again, but I like having a full house. Besides"—the sly smile that matches Colleen's reappears—"I think we have a lot to learn from each other, you and I."

CHAPTER 11
SAM

Gran is punishing me.

I didn't say yes to a place to stay the first time she offered, so she gave my room away. To Diane of all people. Who, despite what my sister says, still hates me. And my grandmother is definitely on Team Diane, because she won't give me her phone number so I can try to apologize again.

Now, two nights later, I'm kicking myself, but I can't figure any way out of the mess I've created. Rentals in Greene County that allow pets are harder to come by than I expected, at least on my budget. If I were still working at Congento, I could buy a place. But I'd also be living in Connecticut and making the world a worse place.

The first night, I tried sleeping on Ethan's couch. It was surprisingly comfortable, but hearing my brother and his girlfriend have sex was, unsurprisingly, uncomfortable.

I really didn't need to know that my big brother whoops like a cowboy when he climaxes.

I could've gone my whole life without that knowledge.

The next night from the bed in Alex's guest room, I

unwillingly learned that Alex, despite being the most taciturn of my siblings, does not shut up during sex. All kinds of dirty words come out of that boy's mouth. Feeling like Goldilocks in a porn movie, I didn't fall asleep until the wee hours. And then Gomer and Alex's dog, Trixie, decided it was playtime the second dawn broke.

All that's to say, I can't stop yawning when I pick up Carlos for yet another ride along.

"What? I'm that boring?" he asks.

"Sorry, man," I say over another yawn. "I'm not getting any sleep. I really need my own fucking place."

After handing over the address to the farm we're visiting first, he tells me that his cousin has a garage apartment coming available in a couple weeks. "Can you hold out that long?"

I blink, my eyes bleary. "Maybe. If I start mainlining coffee."

"Careful there, son. We've got a lot of addiction issues in the county."

Not sure if he's serious or not, I tell him I'll take the place. I don't care what it looks like. Maybe some earplugs will get me through the next two weeks.

At the end of the day, I'm so tired I figure I could sleep anywhere, but when Carlos asks if I'm going to Trivia at Tiddy's, my ears pick up.

"Trivia?" When Diane, aka Cortland1898, blocked me on Trivia Crush, I lost my taste for the app. "I didn't know Tiddy's Bar had trivia. When I was growing up, that place was a dump."

"I'd say it's graduated from dump to greasy spoon. Trivia started up this spring. Latonya's nephew Markus does it. He's pretty funny; calls himself MT Bottles."

"They have food?"

"They make a decent burger. Excellent onion rings."

My stomach growls at the idea. "Maybe I will."

"See you in a few, then," Carlos says.

I stop by the Quick Lick on my way back to Alex's. In addition to a farm, the Quick family has owned the place since it was the kind of general store that everyone visited on a daily basis. As I walk in, I notice that it's had an upgrade too, but the offerings are pretty random. kind of like a hybrid crossing of a Circle K, a Duane Reade, and a deli.

When I ask Ginny Quick, a high school classmate who seems to run the family business these days, if they carry earplugs, she shakes her head. "I could order you some," she says with a feral smile. The only smile she employs, at least in my experience. "Get here in a couple days."

"That'll have to do, I guess."

"I heard you were back in town," she says, leaning over the counter and putting her cleavage on display right next to the Slim-Jims and York Peppermint Patties. "We should get together."

"I'm pretty busy, getting settled in at work and all."

"Where are you working now?"

"I've been with the Cooperative Extension since January, but I just got transferred to this area."

She sighs dramatically. "I have been trying to get my father to bring the CCE in. We are having a heck of a time with the corn rootworm."

"We have all kinds of resources." Backing out because it's impossible to end a conversation with Ginny, I tell her, "Check the website," before slipping out the door.

Back in my truck, I check the time and decide to just

head straight to Tiddy's and get dinner for me and Gomer before trivia instead of going back to my brother's place first. "Maybe if I stay up late enough, I'll sleep through the night."

I swear Gomer rolls his eyes at me.

CHAPTER 12
DIANE

WHEN COLLEEN AND I PULL UP TO WHAT IS PROBLEMATICALLY called Tiddy's Bar and I see Samuel sitting with his cute dog at the one picnic table, my heart does that zig-zag thing again—excitement, immediately followed by the need to flee. Unfortunately, there isn't a seat available inside, so after we get our food, we join him.

He nods at me before turning to his sister. "Think it'd work for me to sleep on Gran's couch tonight?"

"What happened to staying at Ethan's?" Colleen tips her head to the side. "Or Alex's?"

Sam shudders and sets down his sandwich. "I can't talk about it."

Colleen stuffs a handful of fries in her mouth and chews for a moment before answering. "I'm sure Gran won't mind. But that thing's hard as a rock."

An awkward silence follows, broken only by Colleen balling up what looks like a half-eaten sandwich into its foil. "I'm going to make sure our team knows we're here."

I half-rise. "Oh, should I—"

She waves me down. "Nah. Finish up. I'll see you inside."

Great. Alone with Sam. Everything I've always wanted stuffed into a grumpy, confusing wrapper.

He's feeding something to his dog under the table, so I try to just focus on my own food.

"You know," he finally says, eyes on the dog. "Seed banks are a good idea and all, but they're not scalable."

"At least they're not evil. Like your former employer."

"I happen to agree with you." He meets my gaze, his lips pressed together in a flat line.

"Then why did you work for them?"

"I took the job–" He breaks off, pressing his lips together for a few moments. "I took it because it made my grandfather proud. He paid for college, so…"

It's not like I had college loans. My family paid for every penny. Still, I can't stop poking the bear. "So… what? Since he paid, he gets to say where you work?"

His mouth twists to the side, making his perfect face ugly for a moment, like that's how he feels inside. "Pretty much."

"What made you quit then?"

He looks up, his expression unreadable. "You."

I cough out a laugh. "You're kidding, right?"

"I couldn't be more serious."

"You quit because of me?"

"Don't get me wrong, I hated working there. But yeah, listening to your arguments after I'd spewed that bullshit pushed me over the edge." He balls up what's left of his food and stands abruptly. "See you inside."

What is it about me that turns the Bedd siblings' stomachs?

It doesn't take long before I've got new companions at the picnic table, and by the time Tiddy rings a dinner bell, which apparently means the games are about to begin, I've made five new friends. Who needs Sam and his mixed signals? Warning his grandma away from me one minute, claiming he quit his job because of me the next. But when I enter the dim bar and scan the crowd looking for Colleen, my eyes can only find the man I'm trying to pretend I don't care about.

Sitting at a table with a woman draped all over him.

Of course, he's got a girlfriend, Di. A man who looks like he does couldn't stay single for long. Forcing my eyes to continue looking for the person who actually invited me to the bar, I finally find her waving from the back. After meeting the rest of her team, which includes a Big John, a Little John, a Tall Paul, and a Small Paul, none of whom could be under the age of seventy-five, I lean in to ask why she's sitting with a bunch of grandfather types.

She just whispers, "You'll see."

Half an hour later, it's crystal clear.

Apparently, Trivia Night at Tiddy's Bar appeals to all ages. Well, people over twenty-one, anyway. The comedian's jokes are a bit too saucy for kids. Every week, in addition to the usual topics like music, sports, and history, there's a Farmer's Almanac category. The Geezers, which is our team's name, count on Colleen for all the pop culture references and any music released after nineteen ninety-five. Meanwhile, they've got the Farmer's Almanac and history covered. With me chiming in on random other stuff, we mow the competition down like a John Deere over a putting green.

I have to admit that I enjoy watching Samuel's face

turn eggplant purple as his team loses round after round, despite what I know are deep skills on his part. In fact, beating him and Miss Boa Constrictor over there fills me with a smug superiority.

Until it occurs to me: this girlfriend must have *other* skills he appreciates.

CHAPTER 13
SAM

Having extricated myself from Ginny's clutches, I'm settling up at the bar when Gomer whines. Looking down, I see that Diane has sidled up next to me.

"Here to gloat?" I grumble.

"Well, I wasn't going to, but now that you mention it..." She grins, and I swear my knees go wobbly at the sight.

I slap a handful of bills on the bar. "Geezers were on fire. Congrats."

"Thanks." She looks behind me briefly. "Hey, um, I don't want to horn in on your date, but—"

"Date? What date?"

"With your teammate?"

Following her gaze, I realize she's talking about the woman now blowing me a kiss. "You mean Ginny?"

"If that's the one who was whispering sweet nothing in your ear, then yeah."

"First of all, she was whispering answers. That were mostly wrong. Second of all, that wasn't a date."

"Looked pretty cozy."

"Trust me, that's just how she is. We went on one date in high school, and she was making wedding plans the next day."

When Diane looks skeptical, I raise my hands in the air. "As I did then, I made it clear that I'm not the settling down type. Especially now, when my career has me traveling all over. I can barely take care of my dog."

"Right," she says, her lips flattening.

I just stare at her, waiting, and she actually seems to get flustered. Something I'm enjoying way too much. "Did you need something?"

She huffs out an irritated sigh and crosses her arms over her chest. "Colleen ditched me. I mean, she warned me she'd have to leave early because she has an early meeting at school tomorrow, but I didn't want to leave when we were on a roll."

"You didn't want to miss winning, you mean."

"Whatever. In any case, I figured I'd get an Uber, but—"

"They don't exist in Fork Lick."

She glances at a table in the corner. "Apparently, the drunk guy over there drives a cab, but the Geezers said only to use him between nine and eleven a.m."

"So you need a ride back to the house?"

She nods.

"So you can sleep in my bed?"

It's her turn to put up a hand. "It's not an invitation."

"I meant it literally. You are sleeping in my old bed. Or maybe Jackson's. Meanwhile, I'm couch surfing and being treated to the various and sundry sounds of my brothers having sex."

"I did not know that," she says, backing away. "I'm so sorry. I'll… I'll find another place to stay."

I just shake my head. "Gran would never forgive me. No worries. I've got earplugs on order at the Quick Lick." Grabbing my change and leaving a tip, I gesture at the door. "Let's go."

The good thing about being in a small space with Diane: I'm no longer tired.

The bad thing about being in a small space with Diane: It brings back memories. Of that kiss in the elevator. That night at the hotel. That kiss up against the barn.

It seemed like she was into it all three times, but each encounter ended with her walking away. Am I that bad of a kisser? Or does she just hate me on principle?

"Are you coming in?" the woman in question asks.

A "woof" from Gomer brings me to the present, and I realize I drove all the way from the bar to our farmhouse on autopilot. Peering through the windshield, I'm relieved to find all the windows dark. "It looks like everyone's gone to bed. So yeah, I'll sneak in and sleep on the couch."

Diane reaches across the cab to grab my forearm before I can exit the truck. "Why don't you sneak Gomer in, let him sleep on the couch, and take the other twin bed in my —I mean *your*—room?"

I dip my chin and meet her gaze, unreadable in the dim light. "You sure?"

She releases my arm. "I'm not asking you to sleep *with* me. I'm just saying, we're adults. You need a bed. There's an extra one in my–I mean *in your*–" She breaks off, flapping her hand in the air. "In the room in which I am currently staying."

With that, she gives me a tight smile and climbs out of the truck.

So… she hates me, but she's too nice to make me sleep on the couch.

Fine. I can deal with that. It's for the best, really. Neither of us has roots anywhere. Not a good time to get involved. It may be frustrating to lie in bed mere feet from her without getting to touch her, but at least I won't have to listen to other people have sex.

She knocks on the driver's side window, startling me. "You coming or what?"

Letting Gomer out, I grab my backpack but don't get far before Gomer blocks my path. His head lowered, he barks once.

"Oh, you're right. Phone." Reaching back into the cab, I grab it from the console and head for the house.

Diane trots to catch up with us. "What the heck was that?"

"What?"

"That little routine with the dog?"

"Oh." I scratch my head, trying to decide whether I should admit how much I depend on my dog to get through the day. "Remember when we met?"

She smirks. "Hard to forget."

Dousing the ember of hope her comment ignites, I remind myself that she's very clearly said she doesn't want to sleep with me. "And I forgot stuff? Like my… uh, what was it I forgot that night?"

She taps pursed lips as she considers my question. I may have a mind like a sieve half the time, but I'll never forget the glide of that plush mouth over mine.

"Your colleague brought your portfolio, and then I brought you your phone."

Her words bring me back to the here and now, where she and I will not be sharing anything more than air. "Ahh, right. You have a good memory. I do not. Lucky for me, Gomer here was trained as a support dog. Long story short, he flunked out, so I adopted him. Turns out he has skills I need. Mainly preventing me from leaving my crap all over New York state."

Before we mount the steps to the porch, I bring a finger to my lips. "Quiet now, Gomes. Bedtime."

Opening the side door to usher Diane inside, I whisper, "Going to pretend I'm sleeping on the couch so Gran doesn't get mad. At me or the dog." After grabbing a blanket and pillow from the linen closet, I settle Gomer on the couch. "Wake me up in the morning, buddy."

Diane follows me up the back stairs. "He can tell time too?"

"He wakes me up when he needs to go out, which is basically sunup." At the landing, I gesture to the bathroom. "You want to wash up first?"

"Um. Yeah, okay. Let me just grab something to sleep in."

A few minutes later, we trade places and I do my own bedtime routine. When I return, the reading lamp is off. Desire throbs low in my pelvis. I'd love nothing more than to remind her of how compatible we were all those months ago, but I crawl under the covers and sink into the familiar, if lumpy, mattress of my childhood instead.

"Night, Sam."

"See you in the"—a yawn interrupts my thought—"morning."

But when I wake at dawn to the cold nose of my dog, he and I are alone in the room.

She is awfully good at leaving me, that Diane.

CHAPTER 14
DIANE

I'M NOT SURE IF HE'S DOING IT ON PURPOSE TOO, BUT SAM and I manage to avoid each other for the next few days. It hasn't been easy to share a room with a guy with the face and body of Henry Cavill and the brains of Neil deGrasse Tyson, but I keep telling myself that it's for the best. After all, if he found out who I really am, I'd lose what I have here: a seemingly endless supply of content subjects and, even more, the feeling of being a part of the kind of family I've always wanted.

In any case, after the first morning, he's up and out before me. For three nights straight, he's either asleep when I return to the room or gets in long after I'm dreaming about him. Some mornings it's hard to tell if he's been there at all.

It doesn't stop me from wishing he'd kiss me again. Wondering if we could make love quietly enough to avoid waking the rest of the household.

Without things getting messy between us.

But instead of acting on those fantasies, I keep busy with shooting and editing content. When I do see him again, he walks in on Ethel and me. I've been helping her with a secret project, which is just adorable.

"What is that?" Sam asks from the doorway of the parlor.

Ethel slams the laptop shut. "None of your business."

He narrows his eyes at her, then aims that suspicious glare of his at me. "Are you two doing anything illegal?"

I have to suppress a giggle because Ethel's videos are about as far from illegal as you can get. "No, we are not."

"Of course not, Sam. Don't be ridiculous," Ethel says with a sniff, even as she shoots a conspiratorial grin my way. "Diane is just teaching me computer things."

"Then why did you hide it from me?"

She lets that hang in the air for a moment before answering. "Because it's private, female business."

Sam may keep most of his emotions under lock and key, but when he's caught off guard, his face reveals all. Ethel's fib works. He does not want anything to do with anything in the realm of female business when it comes to his grandmother. "Fine. Well, I'm just heading to bed then."

"On the couch?" Ethel asks. Something in her tone makes me wonder if she knows exactly where Sam and his dog have been sleeping.

"Yep," Sam says, shooting me a tight smile. "On the couch. Goodnight."

I hate to admit it, but I'm eager to be in the bedroom when we're both awake, so I fake a few yawns and rush Ethel through saving and backing up her work. Sam is indeed on the couch when I pass by on the way upstairs, but by the time I return from the bathroom, he's in bed. The bed that's far, far away from mine, eyes closed.

When I set a glass on the bedside table, he says, "See you got your ice water."

A shiver runs through me at the flood of memories the word ice triggers, but I make myself get in my own bed rather than get on top of him. Like I want to.

"Even though the nights are getting chillier," he adds, his voice low and inviting.

"You know," I begin, testing the waters. Having sex with Sam, in a houseful of people that includes his grandmother and his sister, is definitely inadvisable. But also irresistible. "It'd be warmer if we shared a bed."

Next thing I know, he's hovering over me in a forearm plank, only a hair's breadth separating our torsos.

A giggle escapes past my lips. "Well, that wasn't very hard."

"I beg to differ," he says, shifting so that the hard length that seems to have imprinted on my vagina presses closer. "Should I leave?"

Before he can move a millimeter, I wrap my legs around his torso, locking my ankles behind his back. "You should not."

All the reasons why we shouldn't do this? I bat them away in favor of reasons we should. "We're adults. We're sharing a room. Who cares if we can't get along in the daylight? If memory serves, we did okay in the dark."

"Better than okay, if you ask me," he says, his voice low and growly. Nosing along my jaw toward the space behind my ear, creating goosebumps as he goes, he whispers, "I've thought about that night every day for the past nine months."

"I've been mad at you for the past nine months." He stiffens, separating our torsos, but I dig my fingernails between his shoulder blades to keep him from going too far. "However, I have made so many friends telling the story. Women never get tired of hearing about guys who are assholes."

Grinning, I slide my hands around to his pecs and run my hands over them appreciatively. He's not as broad or tall as his brothers, but I love his lean, contoured chest and shoulders. "Helps if the guy is wicked hot and super smart."

"You think I'm smart?"

I snort. "What, the hotness isn't in question?"

Dropping his weight on one arm, he uses the other hand to circle one pebbled nipple and then the other through my sleep shirt. "I've got evidence that you're attracted to me."

"Eh." I shrug one shoulder. "Maybe I'm just cold."

"I'm doing my best to warm you up," he growls. "But I think we need to be skin to skin to optimize the results."

After we both shed our shirts, he flips us so that he's on the bottom. Broad palms spread across my back, calluses I don't remember from our last encounter faintly scratching my skin. The flannel-wearing version of Samuel seems to have all kinds of bonuses.

Reaching a hand between us and inside the waistband of his adorably old-fashioned plaid boxers, I pause before I hit the heat seeking missile he's packing. "Wait. You don't have a string of farmer's daughters pining after you all over the state, do you?"

He looks off to the right, lips twisted to the side like he's trying to remember. "Only in the southern tier."

"Why just there?"

"That's my territory. Or it was. Till I got transferred."

I nod slowly as my hand resumes its exploration. "And now they're all in mourning."

"To be honest"—he breaks off with a groan as I grip him and run a thumb over his wet tip—"it's the dog that everyone falls for."

"Poor you." I press his length to my cleft, he cups my ass cheeks under my sleep shorts, and we move together, the friction delicious.

"Yeah, he's the chick magnet. I usually disappoint in comparison." His hands skate up my sides and cup my breasts, tweaking both nipples with his thumbs. "When I was a suit, it was different."

I arch into his hands. "But you were an asshole then."

Sitting up, he pulls me close, cupping the back of my head with one hand and my lower back with the other. "Luckily, I wasn't very good at it."

He reaches between us and slides one finger inside me, then another. "You're very good at this," I whisper. "Almost an expert."

"Takes one to know one."

After that, only nonsense words make it from my brain to my lips as he works me inside and out, hands and mouth seemingly everywhere. And then I'm right on the edge, hanging by a thread. He strokes a spot deep inside I haven't had the pleasure of meeting, and then he stops my shout-moans with a kiss as I fall, shuddering, on top of him.

CHAPTER 15
DIANE

WHO KNEW THAT HAVING A SECRET AFFAIR COULD BE SO HOT? I've never looked forward to going to bed so much in my life. Or waking up, for that matter, since Sam is pretty darn good at taking me to climax no matter the hour. Without even having to get in the car.

Ha-ha—I'm already making Greene County jokes like the locals.

It's not easy to keep quiet, but it's a small price to pay for night after night of secret bliss.

The twin bed is a little small, but the nights are getting cooler, so spending them spooning with a strapping farm boy is no hardship.

I mean, it'd also be fun to be able to snuggle with Sam on the front porch swing or give him a peck on the cheek at dinner, but I get why he wants to keep things between us on the down low. His grandmother seems okay with the fact that his brothers are shacking up with their girlfriends without being married, but I guess she might worry about Sam hooking up with a girl who won't be sticking around.

It's just that all the reasons why I can't plant roots here seem less and less important with each passing day. Yes, I should be traveling to make content for my channel, but I'm the one in charge. Why shouldn't I focus it on one region? Or keep traveling, but have a base to come home to? Where a cute dog and a hot guy in flannel await my return, not to mention weekly dinners with the kind of extended family I've always dreamed of?

It all seems possible, until I picture Sam—not to mention the rest of his family—finding out what my grandfather discovered and the many ways my parents have profited from his work. How could they see me as anything other than a spoiled little rich girl and a complete hypocrite?

I wish I had the courage to publicly renounce my family, instead of creeping around pretending to make a difference with my little nonprofit and my silly videos. But I'd rather pretend I'm doing good than face the truth: I'm just another tiny voice shouting into a howling wind.

Suddenly exhausted, I close my computer without even bothering to check that I've saved the edits on my latest video. Too depressed to do anything useful, I head outside for some fresh air, leaving my camera behind.

The morning was cold and rainy, which is why I've been editing. When I step onto the porch now, though, sunlight filters through the trees lining the driveway, making the leaves glow almost neon green, but I resist the urge to run back inside so I can record the gorgeous view. I need a reset, and diving right back into making content when I'm feeling down won't be productive, no matter how pretty the pictures.

A buzzing noise I don't recognize starts up. Following

the sound around the side of the sheep castle, I eventually find a man bent over its queen, improbably snuggled between his legs, belly up. Ethel perches on a low stool close by, talking to Baabara and whisking wool out of the way as the man clips it. When she notices me, she brings a finger to her lips, indicating that I should be quiet, before waving me closer.

"Baabara's a bit shy when she's being sheared," Ethel explains in a low, soothing voice once I've sidled up next to her. "But Cillian McCarthy's an artist."

The man doesn't look up, just grunts as he turns off the shearers and rearranges the sheep's position, tucking one of her forelegs behind his knee. When he starts up again, he pulls her skin tight with one hand as he runs the clippers over it with the other, leaving behind the smooth, pink skin of her belly and then her flank.

"He's the best shearer in the entire Hudson valley. Oh, and you two might be related. Her last name is McCarthy too, Cillian."

"There're a mess of McCarthys in the world, Ethel." The man's accented voice is gruff, but the laugh lines around his green eyes deepen as he speaks. "Where in Ireland are yer people from, miss?"

I wince. "I'm not sure exactly. I think my McCarthy strain has been in the States for some time. But my grandparents planted an apple orchard south of here."

"Smarter than growin' potatoes," he says with a wink. When he gets the clippers going again, Baabara's skin wiggles, and Cillian mutters something to the sheep.

"Does it hurt her?" I whisper.

"Course not," he says. "She's just antsy. Just a bit more, wee girl."

Ethel quietly drags another stool over and gestures for me to sit next to her. It's oddly soothing to watch the man run clippers over Baabara's curves, the blobs of fiber bobbing to the floor around us, and my worries fade away. An impressive, fluffy pile of wool grows behind the sheep as he twists her body into what looks like sheep yoga positions, shearing the wool from every bit of her body. Ethel has been eager to record the entire process, from sheep to needles, so I'm surprised she's not recording this. "How come you're not filming?" I ask quietly.

She lifts her finger to her lips again and then mouths "I am." Pointing to her phone, which is suspended above the sheep and shearer, she whispers, "I don't want Baabara to be embarrassed, so don't say anything."

Nodding slowly, suppressing a giggle, I give her a thumbs up.

When he's done, Ethel gives the sheep a kiss on the nose and a treat, and then Baabara literally kicks up her heels before cantering away into a field.

Cillian tips his hat at Ethel, which makes her blush again, before bidding me a gruff goodbye and driving away. After Ethel resets her phone on a tripod—the one I gave her when I first visited, fibbing that it was an extra—I hold the bag open while she gathers the wool and stuffs it inside. She explains how she'll skirt and scour the wool before spinning it, and then I suggest she repeat the instructions to the camera.

"You can use that bit as a teaser for your next post," I say.

She wags a finger at me. "Always thinking ahead, aren't you?"

A huge sigh heaves out of me, and Ethel tips her head to the side. "Something's upset you. Is it Samuel?"

"No, no. Sam's been… fine." Not going to get into any more details about him, not with his grandma. Sinking back onto the stool, I shake my head. "It's my family."

Ethel settles down next to me and pats my knee. "Colleen says you grew up in New York City. What got you interested in farming?"

"The orchard my grandparents ran. The one I told Cillian about."

"Ran, as in, they don't anymore?"

"They passed away about five years ago, and it was sold."

"Your father didn't take it over?"

I almost tell her that it was my mother who would've inherited, but I catch myself just in time. Ethel believes my last name is McCarthy. "No ma'am, he didn't."

"I'm so sorry to hear that. I bet you miss them."

I nod, my chin trembling. "I'm the youngest grandchild, and they were a lot older than you are, but I wish I'd had more time with them."

"I'm sure they'd be proud of the work you're doing."

I've been so focused on undoing the damage of my father's side of the family that I never thought about how my maternal grandparents would feel about my nonprofit. "I hope they would," I finally say, my voice thick.

"When I'm missing my Eugene, or my son Jimmy, I imagine them watching out for me from the photos I've got hanging in the house, cheering me on."

I look over to find her eyes shiny as she gazes at the house in the twilight. After a moment, she waves a hand in front of her face. "That's pretty silly, isn't it?"

I take her hand and give it a squeeze. "I think that's pretty cool, actually."

She turns to face me. "Do you have any pictures of your grandparents? Maybe that would help."

"I don't have any prints on hand." Even as I say it, a tightness I hadn't realized was gripping my chest releases, giving me the freedom to take a full breath. "But I think I know where I can get some."

The next day, after our usual early morning wakeup call from Gomer, where hitting the snooze button means giving him a puzzle toy he can enjoy until he alerts us that others in the house are stirring, Samuel uses the time well before scooting down the back stairs.

It takes me a moment to come back to earth, but when I do, I hop out of bed, excited to head south to the Ulster county seat in Kingston. Less than an hour later, I've found even more than I expected—not only the date of my grandparents' wedding, but from the property records, I learn that the orchard is up for sale.

Torn, I pause outside the stately brick building, but after a few moments, I decide I need to find a photo of my grandparents before I visit a realtor. It's unlikely that I have enough liquid assets for a downpayment on the farm, and even if I did, I'm not sure I deserve it.

The faces of my beloved Nana and Pops, however, I do deserve to see again, so I get back in the car and drive up the highway to the largest town near the old farm. There, the West Saugerties librarian gets very excited when I tell her what I'm looking for.

"I'm a bit of a genealogy nut myself," she confesses, rubbing her hands together like an evil villain with a sweet smile. Pulling one of what looks like many pencils from her bun, she gestures for me to join her at the computer monitor in the local history section. Tongue in the side of her mouth as she concentrates, she taps away on the computer, jotting down information on the back of an old card catalog card.

"You're in luck!" After clapping her hands together, she hands me the card. "We've got their wedding pics on the microfiche copies of the old newspaper, but we also have an adorable photo from just ten years ago in the digital version of our seasonal magazine, which means they might even have the original files."

Less than an hour later, my new best friend has printed two photographs for me, and I can't decide which I love more. The wedding picture is beautiful, if grainy—my grandmother's dress trailing gracefully behind her, my grandfather's smile lighting up his whole face. But the color photo from a hilarious magazine contest is a delight. Along with posed couples, including a man and his dog, a same-sex couple, and two babies, my grandparents appear in a re-creation of the classic *American Gothic* painting.

"I'm surprised they won the Most Authentic category," the librarian says. "I mean, their outfits are perfect, but the original painting was supposed to be a farmer and his daughter. Most people just assume they were man and wife."

Even though their expressions are pretty grumpy, I'm so excited to have the print that I give her an impulsive hug. "This means so much to me. Thank you for helping me find it."

As Ethel had predicted, just looking at my grandparents' faces gives me comfort. My mother may have hated growing up "in the middle of nowhere," as she called it, without the advantages of city life or the funds to afford them, but I'm grateful I got to spend as much time with them as I did. And I do think they'd be proud of the work I'm doing, maybe even as excited about it as Ethel seems to be.

My trip to the real estate office isn't quite as inspiring, but I make an appointment to tour the house and orchard later in the week. Even if I can't afford—or shouldn't indulge in—buying it, I can at least visit and take pictures to add to the photo gallery I plan to bring along with me wherever I go next.

Later that afternoon, Sam texts to tell me he's planning to go to trivia and that he'll meet me there after work. Colleen promises to go too, and even brings along Alex and Molly. When I met Molly the first time I visited the Bedd's farm, I thought she had the widest smile I'd ever seen, adorably highlighted by the freckles across her nose. But since she's returned and made up with Alex, she seems to be floating on air.

I try to talk them into joining the Geezers, but I'm informed that we're already at the limit. Instead, Alex and Molly team up with Sam, that woman Ginny, and a couple I recognize as the owners of the local feed store, Chen and Diego.

This week, I'm not as upset by the way Ginny paws at Sam, but I'm even more determined to beat her. Unfortunately, this week's Quick Picks—as Ginny's team is called —are formidable opponents.

The Geezers win the movie round, thanks to Small Paul's knowledge of silent-era film, but the QPs kill us on US geography.

"No fair!" Colleen yells. "Molly just spent the last year driving all over the country."

Our host just rolls his eyes and pulls up the slide for the first question in the Farmer's Almanac round. "What traditional holiday celebrating the harvest takes place on August 1?"

Big John, who has the answer sheet in front of him this round, prints neatly without hesitation, "Lammas Day."

"I didn't know that," I murmur.

"Shhh," hisses Tall Paul, the Geezer who's always worried people will copy our answers.

"Question two," MT intones, "August 8 is National Sneak Some *blank* Onto Your Neighbor's Porch Day."

"That's so easy," Colleen says. "It's—"

"Shhh!" Little John slaps his hand on the table. "Don't say it out loud. We've got it."

Colleen rolls her eyes and mouths "zucchini" to me, like I didn't know.

Our team is sure about the next two answers, but we argue a bit over the final question, "What is the name of the first full moon of November?" We finally write in Hunter Moon, even though Small Paul argues that it's in October.

And when MT reads the answers, it turns out he was right. Unfortunately, the Quick Picks got the correct answer: the Beaver Moon.

"Which means," MT announces, his mic crackling, "We

now have a lightning, head-to-head, tiebreaker round. Our two top teams need to choose their representative."

After a lot of whispered arguments, Colleen convinces the Geezers to send me up to the stage since I came up with half of the answers this evening. There, I'm faced with none other than my very own secret Bedd Fellows Farm bedfellow.

Sticking out a hand, I say, "May the best woman win."

With a wicked smile, he turns my hand over and kisses it. "We'll see about that."

A collective *oooh* rumbles through the room as MT hands us each a buzzer. Just as I'm hoping I can stay focused, Ginny shouts, "Do it for me, Sam!"

Oh, it's game on, Ms. Quick-to-try-and-steal-my-man.

Sam's fast and he knows his trivia, but I've got jealousy on my side. I pull ahead fast with my knowledge of fashion greats and New York Knicks history, but he catches up on herbal tea varieties and local politics—which has Colleen yelling "Not fair" again.

By the time we get to the final question, we've somehow scooted so close together that we're practically nose-to-nose, and when I beat Sam to the buzzer and yell the answer to the question "In what century were potatoes first grown in the United States?"—spoiler alert, it's the eighteenth—Sam howls in frustration before grabbing me by the cheeks and planting a kiss right on my smacker.

Right in front of half of Fork Lick.

"Just because you kissed me in front of everyone doesn't mean we have to be, like, boyfriend and girlfriend," I say the minute we're alone in the cab of Samuel's truck, suddenly feeling like I'm thirteen all over again. "I mean, things don't have to change between us."

Sam just stares at the steering wheel. "Because you're leaving."

"Well, yeah." I say, even though I've been wondering if I really need to.

"But what if I want more?" he asks so softly I can almost tell myself that I imagined it.

When he turns to face me, the naked longing in his expression makes it clear that I didn't. "Um. More what, exactly?"

"Forget it."

He shakes his head and reaches to start the engine, but I grab his wrist before he can. "I mean it. What do you mean by more? I'm not sure if I could have more orgasms in a day, but hey, I'm game to try if you are."

"That's not what I meant, and I think you know it." Collapsing back into his seat, he looks at the roof. "It's not like I'm an expert in the field of dating, but I don't want to hide in the bedroom anymore. I'm sorry that I didn't ask you first. That was probably shitty."

"It was surprising, that's for sure."

"It's not that I want my family or this town all in our business—which they will be now, just so you know. I just want, I don't know… to know more about you. Your family, what you were like as a kid, that kind of thing."

And there's the rub. Swallowing past the avalanche of boulders now lodged in my throat, I push out the words, "What if you didn't like what you found?"

He turns to face me, unruly brows furrowed. Even in

the dim light of the poorly lit parking lot, I can read this expression: total surprise. "I don't think that's possible."

Coughing out a bitter laugh, I scrub both hands over my face. "Oh, I think it's possible, all right."

He shifts, this time torquing his whole torso in my direction, and gently takes my left hand in his. "Try me."

Squeezing my eyes shut, I whisper, "I'm not ready. Is that okay?"

Kissing my palm, he says, "You're not the only one with a past you don't like, you know. So I get it. And I can wait."

"Thank you." Squeezing his hand, I blow out a shaky breath. "So what are we going to say when people ask? About us."

He squeezes my hand, releases it, and starts the engine. "We'll tell 'em to mind their own damn business."

With Sam gone for two days and nights, it's ridiculous how empty the twin bed feels, like we've spent years spooning every night rather than days. Unfortunately, it also gives me time to worry about what I'm doing here. I want him to want me; I want his friends and family to like me. But the more they like Diane McCarthy, the more I worry they'll hate Didi Mayer.

The only good news is I'm extra productive in his absence, finishing up interviews with Ethel's seed co-op and sticking to my content schedule.

Which gives me plenty of time at the end of the week to visit Kaaterskill Orchards, named in honor of my grandmother's Dutch ancestors, and the forest nearby. Now, sadly, it's just called lot ZXT485.

It's a beautiful late summer day, so I take the scenic route and punch in a playlist that reminds me of driving from Vassar to visit my grandparents for the weekend. Lowering the windows, winding down the country roads, my emotions are all over the place. Anxious and uncertain about my growing attachment to Sam, excited and fearful about what I'll find when I get to the orchard. But also blissful because my body and my heart are shouting that I'm heading home.

None of the residences my parents own—not the penthouse Manhattan apartment, not the vacation homes in the Hamptons or Colorado—ever felt like home to me the way my grandparents' farmhouse did.

It's strange, though. I've begun to overlay memories of my grandmother's kitchen with Ethel's. The layouts are similar: bank of windows over the sink, brick wall behind the stove, big wooden table that serves as a work surface, walkthrough pantry that leads to the dining room.

But as I turn onto the county road that leads to the orchard, I realize that the smells are different. Instead of an occasional waft of cow manure floating over from the dairy, the sweet scent of apples fills my nostrils, growing more intense the closer I get. When I pull up the drive, the anticipation of being folded into my nana's arms, of a hair ruffle from Pops is so strong I almost believe I'll see them waiting for me on the porch.

Instead, though, a fancy sedan idles in the drive, its motor running wastefully. After I park, the woman waves to me before turning off her car, stepping out to greet me, and handing me a glossy brochure.

After introducing herself, she picks up our conversation from earlier in the week. "As I said, we have offers on the table, but the seller is accepting them through the beginning of next week. Are you with a developer or… ?"

I'm not sure if she finishes her sentence or not because I'm so shocked at the images on the shiny paper in my hands. Instead of rows of lovingly nurtured heirloom apple trees, I'm looking at rows of cookie-cutter townhouses.

CHAPTER 16
SAM

AFTER A TWO-DAY CCE SUSTAINABILITY MINI-CONFERENCE IN Ithaca, I return to Fork Lick just in time for a Bedd Fellows Farm meeting. We've never had one before, as far as I know. I have no idea what things were like when my parents were alive, but ever since I can remember, Eugene Bedd made all the decisions and Ethan did what our grandfather told him to.

But tonight, Ethan has invited all the stakeholders—Gran and each of us siblings, including Jackson, who will be joining virtually—as well as Lia, who is still serving as our liaison with the lienholder. Diane is hanging out with Molly over at Alex's place for the evening, which makes me a little grumpy because I already missed two nights with her this week and I'm moving out Sunday. Still, I am bursting with ideas from the conference, so the minute Jackson logs on and Ethan calls the meeting to order, I'm literally bouncing in my seat.

Lia presents the financials from the past two months of berry picking. Since much of the outlay for the new crops was covered by grants, the net income continues to cover our monthly payments. But we still need to find ways to pay back some of the principal. When Ethan starts talking about his plans after this year's soybean harvest, I can't keep my mouth shut any longer.

"I know Grandad hated the idea of a whole other round of planting, but the cycles of rain and drought we've had over the past decade, in addition to higher fuel, fertilizer and labor costs, mean that planting a legume cover crop is a no-brainer. Studies are showing that it not only infuses the soil with nitrogen but if you combine that with reduced tillage, you save on energy costs and improve the soil's water-stable aggregates."

Alex places a hand on my arm, and it's only then that I notice Ethan's face turning purple. Even though I haven't even gotten into new ideas from the sustainability conference, I stop talking.

Ethan clears his throat, but instead of just returning to the prepared speech he'd been reading, he says, "It's hard for me to concentrate when you interrupt me, Samuel."

Carlos' voice echoes in my head. *As an outsider, you can never know all the variables. Even on your own family farm, if you're not there on a day-to-day basis.*

Right. I'm an outsider, and I always have been. But instead of that making me mad, I try to accept it as a simple reality. Even though I've been sleeping on the farm for the past two weeks, I'm not the one walking the fields, planting the crops, or putting food on the table.

"I'm sorry, Ethan."

Alex points at a piece of paper sitting on the table. "There's actually a line item on the agenda for new proposals. So maybe hold your horses until then?"

It's not easy, but I do it, clamping my jaw shut,

breathing through my nose and listening. I tamp down the frustrations that my brothers have obviously welcomed ideas from their girlfriends and do my best to stay open to the details of the outcomes to date. When Colleen shares what she learned from her conversation with FarmNet, I don't jump up and claim the idea as my own. When Ethan opens the floor for questions, I find that most of mine have been answered. Collectively, he and my sister and Lia and Gran are doing a damn good job of salvaging the farm.

Just when that they-don't-need-me, outsider feeling raises its ugly head again, Gran turns to me. "I have something I'd like your input on, Samuel."

She describes her planned kitchen garden expansion for the following spring and the issues with growing food near the soybean fields, where Ethan needs to spray pesticides to protect the crop. "I'm not going to even try to get organic certification, that's too expensive, but I do want the food I grow to be safe and healthy. I'd appreciate any ideas you have for alternatives."

Instead of mouthing off about the pesticides or jumping in with half-thought-through ideas for alternative uses of the land near the new garden, I nod slowly. "Let me think on it, and if it's okay, I'll come back to the next meeting with some proposals." I look up at Ethan. "If there is a next meeting, that is."

"This has been very helpful for me, and I hope it has been for all of you, so yes. I think we'll make this a monthly occurrence, if that's okay with you all," Ethan says. When he gets a resounding round of "Ayes," he brings the meeting to a close.

"You get a massage or something? Take up meditation?" Carlos asks the next morning on the way to our second appointment of the day. "You seem more relaxed than usual."

"What? No. Do *you* get massages and meditate?" I shoot back, not sure if he's making fun of me.

"On occasion. Have to find healthy ways to de-stress in this crazy world."

Carlos is the least-stressed person I've ever met, so maybe he's got a point. But I have a feeling that having had athletic, adventurous and probably addictive sex for the past week has something to do with my positive frame of mind. Even though I know this thing with Diane has an expiration date—or maybe because I know that—I'm savoring every sip of her.

Gomer nudges my shoulder, reminding me to focus on what my boss is saying. It doesn't take long to realize that he's talking about the farm we're heading to. He tends to think out loud, and for the first time since we've been working together, it dawns on me that while I may know a heck of a lot about soil science, Carlos knows people.

Also for the first time, I don't say a damn word as we walk the fields with farmer Don Reynolds. Every time my mental chatter starts up–*they'll never listen to me, their ideas are old school, they're too stubborn to change*–I remind myself that even if I'm right about the science, I might not be right about the situation.

When the inner monologue gives up and drops away, I notice a few things. Like I'm wearing comfortable work boots instead of dress shoes that pinch. I'm working under blue skies instead of fluorescent lights that flicker annoyingly. When I take a deep breath, I take in the scents of loam, autumn leaves, and drying hay, instead of burnt coffee and whatever's rotting in the breakroom fridge.

Best of all, nobody's breathing down my neck expecting me to help sell more products like I'm more of a drug dealer than a scientist.

By the time we get back to the truck, I'm not only smiling, I've had an epiphany. As I clip Gomer in, I ask my boss, "Why didn't you tell me you have a formula?"

He grunts as he settles into the passenger seat. "Formula? For what?"

"For working with clients. I just realized it. You do the same damn thing every time."

After I fasten my seat belt, I look up, but he's just staring at me, shaking his head. "No idea what you're talking about."

"You have a formula. I can't believe I haven't noticed it before." I punch in the address for our next stop, eager to get to the next operation so I can try it out myself. Putting the truck in gear, I pull out onto the road. "First, you listen. Next, you answer all of the client's questions. Next, you point out two things they're doing that are working—always two—and your voice has this distinct tone of admiration. Then, you show them the results of the tests we've run, and you give them three recommendations. No more, no less."

I glance over at him at a stop sign, but he's just looking straight ahead, brows furrowed, stroking his beard, so I add, "The thing that I'm curious about? You put the one they really need to act on third on the list. Not first. And you don't tell them there's a hierarchy. Why is that?"

Carlos continues to stare out the window, his weathered skin creased in thought. Finally, he barks out a laugh. "You know, you're right. I had no idea I do that."

"Could've saved us a couple weeks of riding around like this," I can't help but grumble as I pull through the intersection.

"Yeah, but then I would've missed out on really getting to know you." I can't quite tell if he's joking, so I glance over, only to find him staring out the window again. "You know, being neurodivergent can be tricky, but I personally think the strengths outweigh the challenges."

Not quite following the non sequitur, I ask, "Are *you* neurodivergent?" Feeling his gaze on me, I glance over again.

"I'm not, but my nephew is. He's just a few years younger than you and wasn't diagnosed until a couple of years ago. When I was coming up, there was a lot of stigma around anything that was different, so being labeled with a developmental disorder could be really damaging."

The sudden roar in my ears makes it difficult to concentrate. Still, I need to hear his words like I need to take my next breath.

"From what I see in my nephew," Carlos is saying, "understanding more about how his brain works has been freeing for him. Empowering even."

A car honks behind me, and I realize that I've been sitting at another intersection, my hands gripping the steering wheel like it's a horse that's going to run away with me. Gomer's muzzle lands on my shoulder, and I take a deep breath.

My heart still hammering behind my sternum, I look both ways before pressing on the accelerator. And then I make myself ask, "Are you talking about me?"

"Might be something to research," Carlos says like it's no big deal.

Like he hasn't just given the kids who called me a freak, the women who broke up with me because I was difficult, and the grandfather who rejected me justification for their actions. It's not just that I don't fit in here in Fork Lick or with my family.

I don't fit in anywhere.

CHAPTER 17
SAM

IT'S EASY TO KEEP MY MOUTH SHUT DURING OUR FINAL appointment of the day because all I can think about is what Carlos said. When we return to the office, I tell him that I want to do some research on alfalfa pests—the only thing I remember the woman we met this afternoon asking about—but instead, I pull up an incognito search window and go down a neurodivergence rabbit hole.

Twenty-five open tabs later, I'm more agitated than I was before. I don't think I have any of the dyslexias, or Tourette's. But I could have OCD, autism spectrum disorder, ADHD, sensory processing issues, or a cocktail of all of the above. I take a few online tests, but they just get me more confused. So I do the next best thing. Text my sister.

> Me: Did you ever think I was neurodivergent

The dots come and go under her name so many times I almost break down and call her, but I don't want to talk about this out loud at work.

Colleen: Why do you ask?

Me: Give it to me straight Ree

More dots.

Colleen: Okay. After a training at work a couple years ago, it did occur to me that you might be on the autism spectrum or maybe have ADHD. It would have been easy for it to go undiagnosed when we were in middle school because we were going through so much change and grief.

Me: Why didn't you say anything about it

Colleen: It didn't seem important. You're well-adjusted. You're successful. I figured it would just stir the pot unnecessarily.

Colleen: I'm sorry if that wasn't the answer you were looking for.

I just stare at my phone for a long time. Is she right? Am I well-adjusted? Or is Carlos right? Would knowing how and why my brain works differently be a relief? Or would a diagnosis just give people permission to isolate me further?

These questions continue to circle the drain of my brain for the rest of the workday. On the drive home, I try to focus on the world around me. Autumn has always been my favorite time of year. There's something about the quality of the light. Even though it's a crazy time for farmers as they rush to get the harvest in, there's that feeling that everything you've worked so hard for is coming to fruition.

Which, until today, I've been able to relate to. I'm finally loving the work I do and feeling like my hard-won education is doing good. The icing on the cake I didn't realize I wanted? A gorgeous, smart, sexy woman to come home to.

If only it were my home and the woman was sticking around. But maybe it's better this way. The more time we spend together, not only will I get more attached, but the more likely she'll come to the conclusion that every other woman I've dated has. A conclusion that now has a scientific basis. I'm different, and there's nothing they can do to change that.

Anyway, like the seasons, everything comes to an end.

The driveway is full when I pull up to the farmhouse, and I can hardly find a place to park my truck. Gomer's out of the car the minute I turn off the engine, racing off somewhere. Excited barks have me worried, so I hightail it after him.

I can't figure out where the sound is coming from until I realize that it's echoing off Baabara's house. When I finally find him, I can't quite believe what I'm seeing. Gomer's on his back, belly exposed, tongue lolling. Then he jumps up, barking as his front paws hit the ground in a play slap. He and the sheep face off for a moment, and then they race in a circle until Baabara butts the dog and he flips onto his back, which starts the cycle all over again.

My dog is in love with a sheep.

Despite my worries, I can't wait to show Diane. To share this moment with her. To make her laugh. She's usually editing this time of day, so I take the back stairs two at a time to the bedroom. Her computer is there, but she's not. Back downstairs, I follow the sounds of female voices to the parlor and slide the pocket door open a fraction.

Once again, I can't quite believe what I'm seeing.

Ethel Bedd, the woman who in most of my childhood memories is sweating away in the kitchen or being run ragged by five kids, is wiping tears from her bright pink cheeks, and she—along with every other woman in the room—is howling with laughter. It takes me a moment to figure out what's so funny, but when Colleen steps to the side to reveal Diane tangled up in what looks like an entire skein of yarn, I get it.

Diane's got Gran's knitting club under her spell.

Closing the door before anyone notices me, I head out the front door and down the lane to the barn. I don't know why I'm suddenly so angry. Am I jealous? Maybe. But is it that I don't want to share Diane in what little time we have together? Or is it that she so easily fits in around here, while I never have? Not wanting to think about either scenario, I grab the basketball that always sits in the barn office. It's only when I head back outside that I notice the hoop is gone.

I need to throw things right now, and chucking a basketball at a backboard is definitely safer than anything else I could hurl at the moment. Ball on my hip, I search for Ethan, but he's not in the barn or the equipment shed. The tractor's parked, so he's probably not out in the field. Hoping he's moved the basketball hoop to his driveway, I continue down the lane. When I get to his house, I don't see a hoop anywhere, so I bang on his front door until it opens.

Ethan rubs his eyes like I woke him up. "Where's the fire?" he asks grumpily.

"Where's the fucking basketball hoop?" I shoot back, matching him grump for grump.

"I took it down. There's a new one in the barn by the side door. Haven't had time to install it."

"Fine. I'll do it."

Without further ado, I stomp back down the lane. After reading the installation instructions for the new hoop, I call my dog and teach him the words for wrench, tape measure, and bolt, just in case I drop something.

After I locate the studs and drill the pilot holes, it's a little tricky to haul the mounting bracket up the ladder and screw in the lug bolts, but I manage it. I'm just trying to figure out if Gomer could help me get the backboard up the ladder, when a voice startles me from behind.

"What the hell are you doing?"

I catch my balance by grabbing the bracket and the top of the ladder before craning my neck to find Ethan's scowling face. "What does it look like I'm doing?"

"Hanging off the side of the barn like an idiot. And why didn't you put it where the old one was?"

Naturally, Ethan has to criticize the placement of the hoop.

"I thought it'd be better under the side roof. That way we can play when it's raining."

I nearly fall off the ladder again when he agrees with me, but I catch myself just in time. He helps me lift the backboard and then holds it in place—claiming that he's stronger than me—while I screw in the bolts. We hang the net, and while Gomer helps me put away the tools, Ethan looks around with a frown on his face.

"I have no idea where the basketball went."

"No problem. Gomer, fetch the basketball." I have no

idea where I left it either, but Gomer trots around the corner of the barn and returns nosing the ball in front of him.

Ethan jogs over to grab it. Gomer barks, miffed that he didn't get to bring me the ball, so I yell, "Good boy! Come get the tool bag, Gomer."

Happy to have another job, he gallops back, takes the handle in his jaws, and proudly returns the tools to the office.

Ethan shakes his head, but he's smiling. "Game of HORSE?"

"You're on."

It kills me that he barely even has to try to make his shots, just heaves the ball willy-nilly, while I have to go through my whole routine every time. Place my feet, do a mock arc with my hands, three dribbles, and then shoot.

"Overthinking it, like always," Ethan mutters before making yet another easy basket.

Hmm. Overthinking. Is that because I'm autistic or I have OCD? "What happened to the old hoop, anyway? Did it get rusted or something?"

"It was headed that way," Ethan says as he tosses me the ball. "And I realized I could use it to make a grate for the fire pit Lia asked me to put in."

"That's an impressive reuse." Feet, arc, dribble, shoot.

I can't shoot a fucking basketball without going through a ritual.

A grunt from Ethan snags my attention, but his expression's as unreadable as always. "Thanks."

"You should've gone to school for engineering, Ethan."

He narrows his eyes at me, like he thinks I'm making fun of him. "Right."

"I mean it. You're, like, a mechanical genius. That thing you made to plant the strawberry starts? And the changes you made to Gran's basement greenhouse so she can use it all year round? Diane told me how you rigged a clamp so Gran could film Baabara from above. I mean, at the very least you could take some courses at the community college. You could learn how to patent and sell your inventions."

"Like I have time to get to Climax every day."

"From what I heard, you're getting to climax every damn night," I mutter, but he just laughs.

"You're just jealous."

No way am I confessing that I'm getting some too, so I circle back to my original point. "There are night classes. Designed for working people."

He passes the ball to me, hard. "Sam, I was never like you. Sitting in a classroom just made my brain clog up. I figure things out when I'm moving. Driving a tractor, digging in the dirt, mending a fence, even shoveling shit. That's when ideas come. That's how I tease out the solution to a problem."

I'm about to point out that there are accommodations for non-traditional learners, but the irony of it stops me. Biting my tongue, I take my shot, which bounces off the rim. Gomer races for it and noses it back to Ethan.

"Anyway," Ethan continues after taking his own shot, which drops in effortlessly. "I already looked into patents. You can learn anything on YouTube these days. I might file one for my strawberry toboggan."

"That's a good idea," I say, meaning it, as I run after the ball, Gomer chasing me.

Just as I'm lining up to shoot, Ethan says, "You know

the other way I learned? From listening to Pop and Grandad. I know you think they were idiots, but—"

"I didn't say that." I'm too irritated to shoot now, so I dribble a few more times.

"Well, they were old-fashioned in their thinking," Ethan says.

I fumble the ball, I'm so surprised at this admission, but I don't look at him as he continues.

"And I'll allow that they were wrong about some stuff. But they were right about the basics. The… What's that word? Tenets."

I lift a pinky finger and employ the fake British accent we always employ when someone uses a big vocab word or ridiculously correct grammar. "Oooh, fancy word."

"Shut up and give me the ball," he says. "I'm trying to agree with you."

After passing it to him, I remember Carlos and mime zipping my mouth shut. "I'm all ears."

"Pop and Grandad taught me to take care of the land because it'll take care of your family."

It's not easy to keep my mouth shut because I have opinions, but my lips remain zipped.

"They may have been misled by companies like Congento; they may have been operating on now-debunked ideas. But their hearts were in the right place."

I nod because I do believe this.

"Anyway," he says, tossing up the ball without apparent effort. "You and Grandad were cut from the same cloth, so you'd butt heads no matter what."

Letting Gomer run after the ball, I remain still until it seems like he's really finished. "Sounds like you speak from experience."

He snorts. "We're all stubborn, know-it-all assholes, I guess. But we all care about this place."

I can't hold this one in, even though I probably should. "The difference for me is that I care about *all* the places. A lot has to change if we want this land to be here for our kids and their kids to survive. I want to take care of the earth so it feeds people for generations."

"Yeah, well," he says, kicking at the dirt, "we have to get it back from the bank before we can do any of that."

Guilt twists in my gut like colic in a horse. I blow out a breath and do my best to backtrack. "I was going to tell you how impressed I am at how you're running the family meetings, taking in everyone's input before making a decision. I'm sorry I jumped down your throat."

Ethan leans forward, cupping his ear. "Wait. I need to hear that again. I think I heard my stuck-up younger brother admit he was wrong."

"I didn't say I was wrong. I said I'm *sorry*." I roll my eyes. "Sorry you're getting so old you're losing your hearing."

"I may be older, but I'm still bigger and stronger, you string bean."

Before I know it, Ethan's got me in a headlock and is giving me an actual noogie. I'm laughing so hard I can't break away at first, but thankfully, my dog comes to the rescue and side tackles him.

Ethan staggers to the side. "No fair. I don't have a dog."

"That's a *you* problem." I rush to pin his arms behind his back before he can catch his balance. "Take it back."

"Take what back," he says, laughing almost as hard as I am.

"String bean."

"Stuck-up string bean, you mean."

"Gah!" I yell, wrestling him to the ground. We continue to laugh as we roll over and over trying to pin each other.

"What in the Sam Hell is going on out here?"

Sam Hell is the closest thing to a curse word Gran ever uses. In the blink of an eye, we're on our feet and backing away from each other, hands up. "Nothing."

A giggle has my gaze flicking to Diane. She and Lia stand next to Gran, mouths hanging open.

"Nothing, *ma'am*," Gran admonishes.

"Nothing, ma'am," Ethan and I intone dutifully before breaking out in laughter again.

"You two have less sense than the good lord gave a goose," Gran says, shaking her head and turning back toward the house. "I expect you both washed up and in the kitchen to help make dinner in twenty minutes."

Grinning, I pick up the ball and stow it back in the barn office before catching up to Diane, who is scratching behind Gomer's ears. Not sure if it was the basketball or the talk or the wrestling or the laughter, but I feel a billion times lighter than I did an hour ago.

Than I have for a long, long time. Maybe knowing that my brain is different isn't such a bad thing. Maybe it's how I do fit in, rather than why I don't fit in.

I hold out a crooked elbow to Diane. "May I escort you to the house, madam?"

She raises a brow but hooks her arm in mine. "Only if you promise to meet me in the bedroom later." Leaning closer, she fans herself. "Watching you two wrestle? That was hot."

CHAPTER 18
DIANE

WHENEVER I NEED TO THINK, I CLIMB A TREE. THIS crabapple tree on Bedd Fellows Farm isn't quite as inspiring as a Lady Apple or a Northern Spy, but it'll do in a pinch.

Right now, I have a lot of thinking to do, mostly because I can't say no to Ethel Bedd or her grandson. Or is it that I don't want to say no to myself?

The point of creating my channel was to raise awareness around seed saving all over New York state. All over the country, eventually. But right now, Ethel's got me focusing on one town. One hamlet.

Fork Lick has a surprisingly robust community doing a bang-up job fostering local varieties of plants. Every time I think I've exhausted video subject matter, Ethel's got a new idea I can't say no to. Like the video I shot this morning, which I should just give to Ethel to post. Her sheep may be an heirloom breed that provides incomparable wool, but she's no seed.

I need to pack up and move on, but for the first time in my adult life, I want to put down roots. Like the tree I'm perched in. Where I'm wasting time playing a game instead of planning my next move.

"Is this a new camera technique you're practicing? Shooting between the leaves?"

Peering down through the branches, I find Sam grinning up at me. I've cataloged most of this man's expressions over the past week, but that beacon of light and warmth is one I'll never get tired of.

One I'll miss when I'm gone.

His eyes scan the trunk and lower branches, and before I know it, he's clambered up to perch on the branch below mine. "Either this tree shrunk or I'm a lot bigger than I was the last time I climbed it."

"I'm guessing it's the latter."

He plucks a crab apple and sniffs it. "Have you tried one?"

I shake my head.

"Do you dare me?"

What I'd like to dare him to do could be chanted on a playground, but if we get going, we might fall out of the tree. Before I can answer, he takes a bite.

"Yikes! Crab apples are way more sour than I remember too." He shudders, dropping what's left of the fruit like a hot potato, then looks around. "So if not picking apples, what're you doing up here?"

"You caught me with my latest obsession."

"I thought I was your latest obsession." His tone is teasing, but there's more truth to his words than I'll admit.

"Since I've conquered trivia in this town," I say with an imperious sigh, "I've moved on to other subjects."

He points a finger at me. "We'll see about that. There's always next Tuesday."

If I'm still here. Which I shouldn't be. "I thought you were moving to your new place over the weekend."

"I am. But it's only up in Climax. I can still get to trivia."

We haven't talked about what the move will mean to our arrangement. But it's a moot point anyway. As soon as I get my ass in gear and schedule a visit with the next person on my contact list, I'll be gone. Unless I buy the orchard…

"So if not me, what is your new obsession?"

Dragging my thoughts away from the movie that's been playing in my mind since last night of a bulldozer knocking over my beloved apple trees, I hold up my phone. "The World of Wings app. It's a fun way to learn to identify bird species."

After I show him how it works, he pulls up an app on his own phone. "Do you have Merlin? It's run by the ornithological lab up at Cornell."

As he scrolls through his life list, I blow out a whistle. "You've spotted all of these birds?"

"That's the cool thing. Sometimes I can't actually get close enough to see details, but I can record the call, and I identify it that way."

I could sit up here with him until dark, but after a few minutes, he shifts uncomfortably. Peering down, he says, "I don't know how much longer this branch will hold me."

Before he can leave, I reach for his hand. "Sam?"

"Yeah?"

Instead of telling him that I'll miss him when I'm gone, I say, "Can I ask a favor?"

"If you give me a kiss," he says, leaning close.

As I ever so slowly move my lips toward his, I chant

softly, "Sam and Diane, sitting in a tree…" until we're K-I-S-S-I-N-G.

Later that afternoon, after a torrid makeout session in the crabapple tree, and after Sam helps out at Bedd Fellows Farm's strawberry picking, we get to the favor: a soil and water evaluation of the Kaaterskill orchard. But as Sam turns into the drive, I can't stop the gasp that escapes past my lips.

"What's the matter?" he asks, slamming on the brakes.

Taking a shaky breath, I point at the real estate sign. "It's already under contract. The realtor said I had another few days to make an offer, but I guess the sellers changed their minds."

He just stares at me. "Were you actually planning to buy it?"

Swallowing past the emotion clogging my throat, I shrug. "It's not exactly realistic, but I was thinking about it."

"Do you still want me to do the tests?"

I've been chasing my tail over the idea of buying it for the past twenty-four hours, wondering if I can afford it, since I've sunk my entire trust fund into the nonprofit. Could the seed library purchase it? Or is that being too selfish? But maybe the orchard could serve as the center's home base for education and experimentation.

But now, that all seems to be moot.

"We can still run the tests," Sam says, breaking into my thoughts. "You never know what'll happen. Maybe the buyer will back out."

Gomer's whining to get out of the truck, so I nod. "A realtor showed me around earlier in the week," I explain as Sam pulls equipment from the back. "She said it'd be fine if I stopped by to check out the orchard on my own."

Half an hour later, Sam has what he needs, but we spend a bit more time wandering up and down the rows, munching on apples that I hope won't go to waste because of the real estate deal. When we hear a raucous, nasal cry overhead, Sam pulls out his phone and identifies the bird.

"It's a white-breasted nuthatch." He reads from the app, as I peer through the branches trying to catch sight of it. "White belly, gray and black on the back. About the size of a sparrow. Good to have in orchards, apparently, because they'll eat up pests for you."

This reminds me of the bird feeders my grandmother kept outside her kitchen window, and without meaning to, I find myself telling him story after story of my summers here. Of making applesauce, climbing trees, learning to prune.

"I just loved being outside, getting dirty…" I pull an apple from the tree and sniff deeply. "Everything about this place."

Sam sets a hand on the gnarled branch of a Braeburn tree. "It's a beautiful orchard. Could probably use some upgrades, but the trees seem to be in great shape, especially considering how hot it was this summer. But I'll run the tests and get you the results. You know, just in case."

"Just in case," I echo. And as we walk back to the truck hand in hand, dammit if I don't have a vision of the two of us doing this thirty years from now.

CHAPTER 19
SAM

Sunday morning, it's all hands on deck at the farm. I'm not sure if it's the petting zoo Alex has set up, the strawberry ice cream he's selling, or the pop-up craft market Lia and Molly organized, but Bedd Fellows Farms is suddenly the place to be for tourists soaking up the last bit of summer in the Catskills and locals looking for a fun family outing.

Diane spends the first hour interviewing the woman selling honey. Instead of keeping bees on her own property, this apiculturist has boxes all over the county set up on farms that appreciate the work her pollinators do for them. After that, Diane jumps in to scoop ice cream. Meanwhile, I'm driving the hay wagon, pulled by a neighbor's draft horse, so that we can deliver guests to the rows with berries ripe for picking—more fun for them, but it also keeps families from tromping all over the fragile younger plants.

It's a nice break from the week I've had. Between helping out at the strawberry picking and the visit to the orchard, I haven't been able to catch a moment alone with my sister, but she did leave a bag of books and pamphlets about neurodiversity in my truck with a sticky note that just said, "Knowledge is power."

She's probably right, but it's still a lot to process. Instead of worrying about any of the changes upending my carefully planned life, all I have to focus on today is guiding the gentle mare up and down the lane and pointing pickers in the right direction. With Gomer riding on the bench of the wagon next to me, making kids laugh with his goofy dog smile, I can't imagine a better way to spend a late summer day.

Well, I could imagine one better way, but I did wake Diane with my mouth in all her favorite places, so I can't complain. I'm trying not to think about the fact that this time is coming to an end. My new apartment is available tomorrow, so I won't need to pretend to be sleeping on the couch anymore. Diane hasn't said when she's leaving Fork Lick, but she has mentioned that she'd like to finish up a series she started in the spring on vineyards in the Finger Lakes, so I imagine she'll be heading there soon.

"Sam Bedd? Is that you?"

Turning toward the familiar voice, I almost fall off the wagon when I recognize my freshman year roommate. "Josh Harmon? What the fu—" At the sight of the two little kids at his side, I choke back the four-letter word. "What the fork are you doing here? I thought you lived in the city."

"Our mom died, so we live with our grandma and grandpa now," the little girl next to him announces before Josh can say a word. "Daddy lives there too."

"I'm really sorry to hear that," I say to her before mouthing, "Really sorry," to my friend.

Josh gives me a what-are-you-going-to-do shrug before saying, "Mabel is… processing."

"Is that your dog?" the little girl called Mabel asks.

"He is. His name's Gomer." Grateful that she's so easily distracted, I ask him to hop off the wagon. "Do you want to say hi?"

"He's big," she says, eyes wide.

"He is, but he especially loves little girls." I have no idea if this is true, but Gomer loves everyone, so I figure the fib is okay.

"What about boys?" she asks. "My brother's a boy."

Hard to tell what the right answer is here. This is why I shouldn't talk to kids. Before I can come up with something, she crooks a finger at me, so I squat down to her level. "Can you make him bite Percy?"

"Is Percy your brother?"

"Yes. And he's very annoying."

"I don't think I can help you there. Gomer has been trained to not bite anybody." When her lower lip sticks out in a pout and I remember that the kid is practically an orphan, I add, "But he'll definitely give you a kiss."

She immediately puckers up, but before Gomer can lick her on the mouth, Josh deftly turns her head to the side. "Let's keep this kiss rated G, okay?"

Thankfully, she giggles as the dog's tongue swipes over half of her face, and then Josh redirects. "How about that hayride, Mabel?"

"Can Gomer sit by me?"

I raise a brow in question to Josh, who shrugs, so I get them settled in the back. Mabel squeals at every bump in the road, little Percy cackles, and Josh shoots me a grateful smile. At the designated patch, I hand a kid-sized bucket to Mabel and show her how to pick the ripest strawberries and leave the ones that still need to grow. Josh gives Percy another bucket, and the toddler plops down in the lane to fill it with handfuls of dirt.

Once Mabel's worked her way down the row a bit, I say, "I am sorry to hear about Lisa. That's tough."

Josh nods, his mouth in a flat line. "Thanks. My parents have been great, but it's obviously hard on the kids."

He doesn't say anything about it being hard on *him*, but I don't want to pry, so I tell him that I just moved back to the area too. We get caught up on career changes until my walkie-talkie squawks. After a brief exchange with Lia, I explain that I have to go pick up another family. Josh waves me off, saying they'll stay a bit longer, and we promise to get together soon.

As the picking day draws to a close, the neighbor arrives to pick up his horse. After I hand over the basket of honey, jam, and berries prepared by Molly as a thank you, he drives the mare and wagon back to his farm, and I go looking for Diane.

When I find her, she's got a pout to rival little Mabel's.

"What's the matter?"

Stubbing a toe in the dirt, she crosses her arms over her chest. "We sold out of ice cream before I could have any."

Stifling a laugh, I take her elbow and steer her to the barn office. After opening the freezer, I pull out a small container. "Lucky for you, I know where there's a secret stash."

My reward of a kiss takes so long that the ice cream

softens, but I'm not going to complain. After grabbing a spoon from the kitchen, I lead her up the hill.

"Where are we going? The ice cream's melting!" Diane grumbles.

"It'll be worth it, you'll see."

At the top of the hill, we round a boulder, revealing the bench my father built for my mother before I was even born. Gesturing for Diane to sit, I point west. "Best view of the sunset for miles."

Settling on the bench next to her, my arm around her shoulders, I lean back with a sigh and just listen, which I'm getting better and better at. The buzz of insects, the whistle of wind through the trees, Gomer panting at my feet, Diane's moan of pleasure.

"No wonder people are driving for miles to get this stuff. It's amazing."

"Do I get a taste?"

She grumbles about having to share, but she tips a large spoonful into my mouth. "Wow. That is good."

I'm not usually a fan of strawberry ice cream because I don't like the way the berry chunks turn into frozen lumps. But there are no chunks at all here, just the creamy goodness of a vanilla base, run through with a bright acidity from the strawberry puree.

Passing the pint back and forth, we watch the colors chase each other across the sky as the sun sinks toward the mountaintops in the distance. Soon the leaves will be turning, making this view even more dramatic, but I'm happy to be here right now, sharing space with this woman. An image flashes in my mind of me and Diane sitting on a hill looking over our own farmhouse and land, somewhere down the road. It's a beautiful picture, but I do my best to appreciate what we have because there's no way this can last.

"There was the cutest little girl at the market today," she's saying. "With the most amazing blond, curly hair."

"With her dad and little brother?"

She shifts to face me. "You saw them too?"

"I know them. Well, I know the dad. We were college roommates." I wince, thinking about what Mabel said. "Unfortunately, he's a widower now."

She gasps, her hand going immediately to mine. "Oh, no. The kids are so young. And that must have been hard for you to hear."

It takes me a moment, but then I realize what she means. "Yeah. They still have him, but it is really sad."

After giving me the last spoonful of ice cream, she sets the container and spoon on the bench next to her and snuggles in under my arm. We don't say anything more; we don't need to. It feels right to just be together on this perfect summer day, even when the world isn't perfect.

I hate to break the spell, but I don't have a flashlight, so we have to head back down the hill before the sun disappears completely. Gomer's been quiet, and he walks calmly at my side as we head back to the house.

"Does Gomer not like me?" Diane asks, seemingly out of nowhere.

"What? Why would you think that?"

"I've just noticed that he greets everyone you interact with, just noses right in and demands to be petted. But he doesn't do that with me. He kind of ignores me."

"When he first saw us kissing by the barn, he didn't ignore you."

"Right, he got between us." She sticks out her lower lip in that pout again. "I don't think he approves of me."

Not wanting to simply reassure her unthinkingly, I picture the ways that my dog interacts around different people, from strangers to acquaintances to family. "You know, I think it's the opposite. I think he ignores the people he's decided are safe for me."

Her lips twist with skepticism. "Don't try to make me feel better. I don't need your dog to like me."

"I mean it. He also ignores Colleen and Carlos." I stop in the middle of the path between the fenced garden and the house, and Diane does too, turning to face me. Gomer ticks his gaze back and forth between us and then just lies down. "Since he was supposed to be an alert dog for an epileptic, his observational skills are top notch. He's very good at picking up all kinds of things going on with me."

Diane tips her head to the side. "Like what?"

This is veering into dangerous territory because I'm starting to wonder if Gomer has ended up working as a service dog after all. Not for an epileptic, but for a person with a mental disorder. It's scary, but it hurts that she thinks Gomer's judging her, the same way it hurt when my sister asked if I hate my family. It never occurred to me that by protecting myself, I was pushing them away.

I'm not quite ready to drop Carlos' truck seat diagnosis on Diane, but I need her to understand this. Understand at least a tiny corner of *me*. "Gomer doesn't just help me by carrying tools and finding keys. He's like an emotional ice breaker. By approaching people before I can, he distracts them until he knows I'm comfortable. Mostly, that just looks like him being a friendly dog. Only once did he growl at someone, and I learned later that the guy was abusing his wife."

"But he got between us at first," she says, obviously still concerned about how the dog feels about her.

I squeeze her hand, hoping to reassure her, but also to calm myself. "Other than a brief hug, he'd never seen my hands all over someone before. I think it took him a minute to figure out that I liked it."

She narrows her eyes at me. "So none of those southern tier farm girls got a taste of you?"

After taking a brief taste of her, I whisper, "I think you know that those girls don't exist."

She bumps hips with me, grinning briefly. Then, eyes on the dog as he trots ahead of us, she sighs. "I don't know. I don't get why he doesn't even greet me."

"He's figured out that I don't need him around you, so he checks out. I even found him playing with the sheep the other day."

She looks down at him, her brow furrowed. "What would he do if I initiated contact?"

I shrug. "Let's find out."

After I call Gomer back, Diane squats down and holds out the back of her hand for him to sniff. After a nod from me, he bumps his nose under her hand, and she follows the prompt to stroke the top of his head. After she's done that a few times, he rolls onto his back, tongue lolling, and barks.

Diane laughs as she rubs his chest. "He's pretty good at asking for what he wants."

"He could teach us all a few lessons, for sure."

After a good rub down, Gomer flips back over and shakes himself before ambling toward the house again.

I help Diane up from the ground. "You believe me?"

"I don't know much about dogs, but I guess it makes sense."

My belly's a little skittery from the sugar in the ice cream or from opening up my brain to Diane, or both, so I change the subject. "Hey, did you hear anything from the realtor today? About the orchard?"

"She hasn't called me back. Not sure if that's a good thing or a bad thing."

"Do you think you'd try to buy it if it becomes available again?" The orchard is about a half an hour south of Fork Lick, which is another half an hour south of Climax, where my new apartment is. But if she settled there, we could still see each other.

"I don't know. All of my best childhood memories took place there." Sticking her hands in the back pockets of her shorts and kicking at the dirt as she walks, she suddenly looks like a little kid. A lonely one. "Unlike the rest of my family, I hated living in the city."

I basically know nothing about her past beyond the fact that she went to the same college as my sister. Except for the memories she shared in the orchard she's never said anything about her family or where she grew up. To be fair, nearly all of our time together the past week has been naked and between the sheets. Or going head-to-head at trivia.

We've just barely scratched the surface, but I've never felt so close to anyone in my life.

I already asked for more, but she put me off. If I do it again, it might push her right out the door. And there's this neurodivergent thing. What if she decides I'm more trouble than I'm worth, like every other woman has?

Thing is, without any good reason to, a tiny seed of hope has planted itself in my heart. One that says a diagnosis that leads to therapy could be a good thing, make me easier to live with or, at the very least, more comfortable in my own skin. And then there's what I'm learning from Carlos. Maybe, just maybe, if I just listen, without making any of my own demands, I can find a way to get her to stick around.

CHAPTER 20
DIANE

IT'S RIDICULOUS HOW MUCH I MISS SAM WHEN HE MOVES OUT, but it's probably for the best. Not that I do what I really should and leave town, however. Telling myself that I have to stick around for one last chance to win trivia night with the Geezers, I spend two days running all over Fork Lick shooting background footage to cover the bases when I do the final edits.

Unfortunately, from the roadside stand selling locally made preserves to a tractor scaling a hill at sunrise, everything my camera records just makes me want to stay. Even Baabara stopping traffic when she escapes from her pen tugs at my heart.

Tuesday night, when I join the Geezers at their usual table and let them know Colleen won't be joining us, Big John frowns. "Who's going to answer all the pop music questions?"

"Yeah. And the Disney crap," Little John adds.

I wince. "Sorry guys. I've got you on literature and history but—"

Just then the door opens, letting in a gust of cold air, as

well as the man never far from my thoughts. "Don't worry guys. I've got it."

Rushing to meet him, it takes everything in me to keep my hands to myself. "Want to be on my team?"

Shucking his jacket, he tips his head to the side, grinning. "Do you want me for my pop culture knowledge or… did you miss me?"

"Both," I say, unable to keep a silly grin off my face. "Colleen's not here, so we need you."

"Then I'm all yours."

When we show up to the table, Tall Paul scowls. "What good is this guy? We need Colleen."

"I've got you covered," Sam says, hand over his heart. "As her twin, I was forced to watch every Disney movie and Nickelodeon show and memorize the words to every girl anthem right alongside her."

"He doesn't listen to country in his truck." Lowering my voice, I add, "He listens to top forty instead."

Small Paul shudders. "Top forty?"

Big John slaps the table. "You're in."

Sam is as good as his word, and we smash the Quick Picks. Even better, he never stops touching me the entire night. Whether it's an arm across the back of my chair, his fingers playing with my hair, a squeeze of my hand when he gets excited about knowing an answer, or a full-on kiss to the mouth, I have to stop myself from climbing in his lap so I can feel even more of him.

Buzzing with giddiness and humming "New Romantics"—Sam's encyclopedic knowledge of Swift lyrics never ceases to amaze me—I don't even notice another human in the bathroom until I step out of the stall and up to the sink to wash my hands. Not until Ginny hands me a paper towel.

"Oh, hi, Ginny. And uh, thanks." After drying my hands, I throw the balled-up paper away before turning back to her. "Good game tonight."

She just rolls her eyes and crosses her arms over her sparkly shirt. "I may be just a dumb hick who works at the Quick Lick, but I know fashion, Didi Mayer."

"Wh-what did you say?"

"I knew it." Her smile is so slow and smug, I almost expect her to twirl a mustache. "Your name isn't really Diane McCarthy."

"How? I mean—"

"Come on. Nobody actually from this part of New York wears Fendi t-shirts and Vivienne Westwood jeans. We couldn't even afford J. Crew or Madewell." She rolls her eyes. "Like they carry those lines at Walmart. Uh-uh, only big city transplants drop cash on clothes the way you obviously have. I took one look at you and I knew: You're trying to fit in somewhere you don't belong. What I couldn't figure out is why you'd want to." Tapping her chin, she begins to pace the small space between the sinks and stalls. "Then I noticed that your face never shows up in your videos, which made me wonder, is she hiding something? Or from someone?"

She spins to face me and stops to wag a finger back and forth. "Too bad for you, I have a vested interest in finding out and a whole lotta time on my hands. Hardly anybody shops at the Quick Lick anymore, not since the damn Amazon fulfillment center opened up in Coxsackie and you can overnight anything you need. So I have plenty of time to search on the internet, and looky what I found."

Like a detective in a cheesy movie, she whips out what looks like a Xerox of a newspaper photo and gazes back and forth between it and me.

"Didi and Hermann Mayer, Jr. Mm-mm-mmm." She peruses the picture as she hums. "I still don't know why you changed your name. Maybe you're running from a messed-up marriage to this Hermann guy, but it won't be long until I find out. And believe you me, whatever I dig up, I'll tell the entire Bedd family, starting with your beloved Samuel, not to mention the whole damn hamlet. Not only do I have spies, I have ways of getting out the word, you see."

Carefully refolding the photocopy, she tucks it away and pats her bag. "Unless you pack up your Gucci bags and get out of town before dawn, that is."

I have no words, but just in case I did, she leans in, poking my breastbone with a pointy, pink-tipped fingernail.

"And before you try and tell me that you and Sam were made for each other, don't forget that I have something you don't have, no matter how much money you've got. I've got a centuries-old family farm, right down the road. One that he can help me run when we get married so he can move back home where he belongs."

Stepping back, she wags that finger back and forth.

"And. You. Don't."

CHAPTER 21
SAM

BEFORE MY DOG CAN WAKE ME WEDNESDAY MORNING, MY phone does. Seeing my grandmother's name pop up on the screen, I answer immediately. Ethel Bedd never calls her boys just to chat. "Hey, Gran. Everything okay?"

"No, everything is not okay," she says, sounding very upset.

This has me sitting up, heart pounding. "Are you hurt?"

"Yes. I am very hurt. When I went downstairs to make coffee this morning, I found a note on the kitchen table. Do you know anything about it?"

Wondering why she thinks I'd leave her a note, I tell her no, swing my legs out of bed, put the phone on speaker, and head to the kitchen to start my own coffee.

"Are you sure?" she asks.

"I swear, I didn't leave you a note."

"The note is not from you."

Obviously, I think as I begin to fill the carafe with water.

"It is from Diane."

At the sound of her name, alarm bells go off. Hands shaking, I turn off the faucet. "What does it say?"

"It's a very lovely letter thanking me for my hospitality—someone raised that girl with excellent manners—and apologizing for leaving without saying goodbye. She says"—paper rustles and Gran clears her throat—"'I have other obligations I've ignored for far too long, so I'm afraid it's time for me to move on.'"

What the hell?

"Did you say something or do something that would drive her away?" Gran asks.

"No, ma'am, I promise." Sitting heavily at the counter that divides the kitchenette from the living area, I go over the previous night in my head. "We met up at trivia, then I drove her back to your place, said goodnight"—I, of course, leave out the heavy petting that ensued in the cab of my truck until Gomer tried to get involved—"and then went back to my apartment."

"And why didn't you ask her to stay at that apartment?"

My grandparents did an amazing job raising us, but we did not talk about sex or even relationships. I'm pretty sure Gran knows that Ethan and Alex sleep with their girlfriends, but no one has ever acknowledged that in front of her, as far as I know. "Um, because she's been staying with you."

"Well, she isn't anymore," Gran snaps.

"Gran, you know she was going to leave eventually. She has plans for her channel."

"Is that what you want?"

It's probably a terrible idea, but I find myself admitting

to her what I haven't been able to admit to myself. "Of course not. But I can't do anything about it."

"Did you tell her how you feel about her?"

"Um... What do you mean?"

"It's obvious there's something special between the two of you."

"It is?"

"Samuel Daniel Bedd. Stop being such a numbskull. Why do you think I let your damn dog sleep on the couch for the past two weeks?"

"You knew about that?"

"Of course I knew, Samuel. I have eyes in my head, and you don't shed. But I wanted to give you and Diane time to figure out that you're perfect for each other." She sniffs. "And Gomer is very good at fetching things. I kind of miss him."

Gomer barks, hopping up from the floor where he'd been curled at the feet of my chair, and snuffles at the phone, probably trying to tell her he misses her too.

And then it hits me.

I might never see Diane again. Sliding down to the floor, I put my arm around my dog. How could I have let her go?

"Well," Gran says, "it's obvious what you have to do. Find her and convince her to come back."

"I can't do that, Gran," I say, the back of my head thudding against the counter behind me.

"Of course you can. We'll help you."

"No. I can't," I argue, even though I want to. More than anything.

"So you do hate it here?" she asks softly. "You're not planning to stay?"

"No, Gran. That's not it at all. I love it here," I say, realizing how deeply I mean it as the words leave my mouth. "But I can't ask her to come back because it will kill me when she leaves again."

"But she might not leave. Especially if you do a good job of convincing her to stay."

"She will." My throat tight, my jaw tighter, I push out the words I need to make her understand. "Just like Mom and Dad did."

"They didn't leave you, Sam," she says softly, but firmly. "They were taken from us. It was an accident. A horrible twist of fate."

I hate hearing these words. The words that everyone used. When I knew the real story. "What if it wasn't?"

"Wasn't an accident? We know it was. The police reports—"

"What if it wasn't fate?" I grind out. "Or random? What if it was because of me?"

There's a pause, a short one, but she definitely hesitates before asking, "What are you talking about?"

"I begged them to come home early, because I'm selfish," I say, needing the words to be outside of me. Needing to release them from the tiny cage where I've held them so tightly and for so long. "I wanted to feel special because it wasn't enough that they sacrificed so much for us. I asked them to drive back in time for the Science Olympiad just because I'd been invited to compete in more events than anyone else in the school. And they did. They left that night instead of waiting till the next day. And then they never came home."

Tears blur my vision. Or maybe it's the way I've

pressed my fists into my eyeballs. "It's my fault they're dead. I told them I needed them, and that killed them."

"Oh, Sam," Gran says, her voice high and breathy. "I'm so sorry you've been carrying this. I'm sure they wanted to be there for you. They were so proud of you. But—" She breaks off and clears her throat before continuing. "There was a problem with the hopper on the grain cart. Your grandfather was very frustrated and told them about it. We've always thought they decided to come home early because your father wanted to help fix it. He was so much better with the machinery, the way Ethan is."

She blows out a long sigh. "Your grandfather felt guilty about it for the rest of his days. I sometimes wonder if it may have colored how he treated you kids. He may have kept you at a distance because of it."

The way I have, is what I think. But what I say is, "I thought he resented having to take care of us."

"Oh no, honey. That I know for sure. And to be honest, I don't think that either the science contest or the hopper was the primary reason they decided to leave early."

When she doesn't continue, I stare at the phone, squeezing it like that will make her keep talking. "What was it then?" I whisper.

"I found something after your grandpa died. I wasn't sure whether to share it or not. But it might make you feel better. It was a note from your mom to your dad. She wrote him a poem and drew a little picture, telling him that she was pregnant again and she couldn't wait to get home and share the news. It was dated the day they headed home."

Before their car was crushed by a runaway semi.

"So it wasn't your fault or your grandfather's," my

grandmother says, her voice sounding far, far away. "Or anyone's, really. It was just… a terribly sad accident."

Gran musters the troops, and my entire family gathers for breakfast less than an hour later. Before we begin the brainstorming session, Gran places a hand on mine. "I have to apologize to you, Sam."

For a moment, I think she's going to bring up everything we talked about on the phone. As much as I want to be up front with my siblings, I'm not sure I'm ready for that.

"I overheard Jane on the phone telling Ginny Quick personal things about you and Diane right after I talked to you this morning." She shakes her head, clicking her tongue. "I sent her packing. So you were right to be concerned about her."

"Actually, it was Colleen who had a feeling about her," I say. "But thank you. I guess Ginny might've been jealous."

"Going forward, I will certainly get references and get Big John to run a background check before I let anyone else stay here. Luckily, Hetty is a jam-making fiend. It'll be hard to replace her when she goes back to college." She claps her hands. "Now let's get to it. How is Sam going to win Diane back? We need a grand gesture for the ages."

They come up with some excellent ideas, but nothing seems right. Not naming Baabara's next lamb after her, nor building her an editing suite off the pole barn, nor promising to bring her breakfast in bed for the next ten years. My gut tells me that I need to do more than show up with a declaration of love and grovel for being an idiot and not telling her sooner, so I thank my family for the input and promise to tell them what I decide.

Something's eating at Diane, and I think I have to figure out what it is before I can make a successful argument for why we can be together. The problem churns in the back of my mind all morning as I drive along the southern edge of Greene County from one appointment to the next. But it's not until I crest a hill giving me a view of row upon row of apple trees that it finally hits me.

Her grandparents' orchard. The loss of it to a developer must have upset her more than she admitted. Maybe she's ashamed that she didn't have the money to save it?

It's easier than ever to keep my mouth shut during my final farm visit of the day because I just want it over with. I write down every question, every detail the feed corn grower says—because there's no way I'm going to remember this conversation—take soil and water samples, and hightail it out of there so I can get to Kaaterskill Orchards before sunset.

Something tells me that I'll find inspiration at the place where Diane was the happiest, and I make it there just as the sun's flirting with the curves of the Catskills to the west. Walking around the multi-gabled farmhouse set on a rise, so similar to my grandmother's house, I try to picture Diane as a kid. She probably didn't spend her summer days thinking of ways to get back at bullies when the school year started like I did. Did she shell peas with her grandma on the porch? Pick wildflowers that they'd arrange in a milk bottle? It's hard to picture now, with annuals stuffed in pots and bright pillows on the porch glider, out of place for a working farm and likely placed by the realtor for show.

It's only when I turn to face the orchard that I remember: Diane climbed trees. So, Gomer at my side, I wend my way down the lanes created by the neatly planted rows of apple trees, hoping that a walk in a place she loves will help me figure out what to do.

I'm lost in thought, going over the past two weeks, when Gomer stops so abruptly I almost trip over him. Head cocked to the side, he stares into the branches of one of the larger apple trees and whines softly.

And then I hear what's caught his attention: the staccato rap of a woodpecker's bill. Pulling out my phone, I open the Merlin app and edge closer to the tree, peering up through the branches. I catch a flash of red and white, but it's too high up to get a good photo with my phone, so I start the sound recording. Moments later, the drilling stops, and the bird lets out a high-pitched *kwee-ahh*.

When I hit the button, the app identifies the bird as a Red-headed Woodpecker with 98% certainty. The photo that pops up shows a red head and a white breast, tracking with the colors I saw when the bird jumped from branch to branch. After I hit the button confirming that "This is My Bird," instead of the burst of confetti I usually get when I add a bird to my life list, my phone rings with an unfamiliar number.

I'm so discombobulated that instead of sending it to voicemail like I usually would, I answer. "This is Sam Bedd."

"Hello, Mr. Bedd. My name is Jessica Ward, and I'm calling from the Cornell Lab of Ornithology."

Looking around, feeling like I'm being watched, I say, "Okay?"

"Sorry to bother you, but we are monitoring sightings of the Red-headed Woodpecker. Do you have a few minutes to talk?"

Following her prompts, I forward the recording I made to her and then answer all her questions about what I've seen of the bird and the location.

"Is this your property, sir?"

"No, uh, my girl—" I falter, realizing that I can't really call Diane my girlfriend if I don't even know where she is. "Um, a friend of mine grew up here, but the property's for sale."

After walking back to the driveway, I read off the name of the realty company, adding, "It's zoned for development, so the orchard may not be here for long."

"Oh, hell no," the woman says under her breath. "Um, can you hang on for a few minutes, please, Mr. Bedd? I may have some more questions, but I need to talk to my supervisor."

I settle on the porch steps to wait, but the moment Gomer rests his head on my thigh, Jessica is back. "Thanks for waiting. I think that's all we need. We appreciate your cooperation."

"Hey, uh, I actually work for the CCE. Can you tell me what's going on?"

"Oh, cool." She asks what division I'm in, and we chat a bit about her research. "Most people don't want to hear the nitty-gritty, but we'll be filing a stay on that property sale so the Bureau of Wildlife can sue to change the zoning. The Red-headed Woodpecker is on the endangered list. That orchard's not going anywhere."

CHAPTER 22
DIANE

It's only been two days since I left Bedd Fellows Farm, and I miss it and the man I've been sharing a bed with way more than I should. It's not my farm, the Bedd's are not my family, and Sam isn't even really my boyfriend. We just shared a couple of steamy weeks in the sack.

As well as months of Trivia Crush.

That company should start a dating app.

Unfortunately, my mood has bled into my videos, which are as washed out as the rain-soaked barnyard I'm shooting at the moment. My camera is positioned in the doorway of a storage shed across from a barn. The couple who works this organic vegetable farm are packing CSA boxes as well as produce they'll take to a farmer's market early Saturday morning. By shooting through the rain, I was going for a cool, moody effect like Li Ziqi creates on her channel, but what I've got so far is more *in* a mood. A bad one.

We got a few usable shots before the farmers finished packing and retreated to the house for lunch. They invited me to join them, but I don't think I can handle the peopling that would require.

Which has never happened to me. I'm always up for getting to know new people. But leaving the Bedds broke something in me, made me feel more alone than I have since my grandmother's funeral.

I'm about to pack it in when suddenly a door slams, a cat comes running down the lane, and a chicken takes off flying. With the wide lens set up on the camera phone, I manage to catch the chaos on film, including the moment that a donkey pops his head around the corner, tossing it as he brays loudly.

Then, a familiar face fills the frame.

Straightening, his name's on my lips with a wing and a prayer. "Sam?"

The rain picks up, but he just stands there, the corners of his mouth tipped up as he raises his arms to the side. "I'm so glad I found you."

My thumbs clumsy with shock, I almost knock over the tripod as I stop the recording on my phone and swipe the app away. Taking only a moment to straighten the tripod while my heart beats heavily with the words *bad idea, bad idea*, I make myself step around the camera and face him. "What are you doing here?"

He looks a little hurt, even drops his gaze to his feet for a moment, but then he takes a deep breath and faces me. "I couldn't let you leave without knowing."

I want to wrap all my limbs around him, but I shouldn't. Can't. Especially since I can only imagine what he now knows. "Knowing what?"

He shakes his head slowly, his eyes taking me in like he's been assigned to map my face. "That I love you. That

I've had a crush on you since we met on Trivia Crush, that I've been obsessed with your body since that night last year, that I've fallen head over heels for you over the past two weeks."

"But Sam—"

He raises a hand to stop my objections. "I know. I know it's only been two weeks. But it's not just about the sex, and it doesn't matter that I don't know everything about you. I get you. You get me. We care about the same things, you challenge me to be a better person, and you inspire me."

The sky really opens up, and Sam's not even wearing a raincoat, but he doesn't seem to notice that he's getting soaked to the bone. "And it's okay if you're not ready to say the same to me. I'm learning to be patient."

It's my turn to look at my feet. If I don't, I think I'll cry. How can I say no to this man? Worse, how can I say yes and then watch that love turn to hate when he learns everything about me.

Unless…

"Did you talk to Ginny?"

"Ginny?" His brow furrows like he truly doesn't remember the woman who drove me out of town, before it dawns on him. "You mean Ginny Quick? Diane, I told you, there's nothing between us. There never has been."

"So she didn't tell you anything? About me?"

Now he looks really confused. "What would she tell me?"

It wasn't enough, obviously, to sneak away. To hide until the Bedds forget about me. To hope that their memory of me would never be tarnished by the truth.

"She threatened to tell you who I really am if I didn't

leave town. But I guess that was cowardly of me. I'm sorry. I should've told you myself. I was just afraid that if you found out, you'd hate me."

"Hate you?" He takes a step closer, and it takes all of my strength to stand my ground. "Who you really are?"

Nodding slowly, I make myself say the name I legally changed when I turned eighteen. "My real name is Diane Mayer. Growing up, everyone called me Didi. Didi Mayer. And my grandfather's name is Hermann Mayer."

I see the moment that it clicks, and as I predicted, Sam takes a step back. "As in, *the* Hermann Mayer? The father of the GMO? The guy who betrayed his research partner and sold out to SynAgro?"

"Now Mayer-SynAgro. But yes, that's him. That's my family. That's what I come from."

"Why the heck did Hermann Mayer plant an heirloom apple orchard in West Saugerties?"

It takes me a moment to catch up with his logic. "That was my other grandfather. Sean McCarthy. The one who passed away. Dr. Mayer's still living. In a fancy retirement village on Long Island. He's never planted a tree in his life as far as I know."

"Ohhh. That makes more sense." His brow furrows even more. "So why am I supposed to hate you?"

"Isn't it obvious?" I scoff. "Because I'm not poor little Diane McCarthy just scraping by with her little video channel and nonprofit salary. I'm debutante and trust-fund baby Didi Mayer who was raised with every privilege you can imagine and more, all funded by investments seeded by the money my grandfather made selling out to SynAgro."

"But I still don't get what this has to do with you and me."

My arms flap at my side like the chicken I just captured on film. "Because I'm a hypocrite? I vilified you for just working for Congento, while my grandfather made its existence possible."

"Exactly," Sam says, stepping closer and reaching for my hand like I'm a horse who might shy away at the slightest provocation. "Everything you've told me is about your grandfather. Not you. As far as I can tell, you're not living high on the hog off of what he did. You didn't choose to be handed a trust fund. In fact, you wouldn't even let yourself buy Kaaterskill Orchards back."

"Not that it would've made any difference. I was too late."

"Yeah, about that," he says, squeezing my hand. "Remind me to tell you something."

"Tell you what?"

He places his free hand over his heart. "I need to tell you this first. I get how heavy guilt can be, even if it isn't all yours. I've been carrying its weight since I quit Congento."

"You felt guilty for quitting? Why?"

He drops my hands and places both of his on his hips, blowing out a breath. "Because it led to a fight with my grandfather. By quitting, I'd wasted his investment in me. Our last words to each other were angry ones because he died less than a week later."

This time I reach for his hand to hold in both of my own. "I'm so sorry, Sam. That must've made you feel awful."

He meets my gaze, his blue eyes dark with pain. "It

gets worse. A couple weeks ago, I found out that he lied to me. He offered to cover my college and grad school expenses, to fill in the gaps between my scholarships and stipends and the actual cost. He told me I didn't need to take out student loans because he'd had a banner few years and could afford it. But he just took out another mortgage on the farm, putting us even further in debt."

I squeeze his hand. "But you didn't know."

Flipping my grip, he squeezes back. "Exactly. It took a couple weeks of beating myself up, but I finally got it. It was his choice. Just like your grandfather's choices were his. Not yours."

The moment he finishes, the rain stops. Looking up, I watch as the clouds overhead lighten as a ray of sunlight slants between them.

"Oh, also, I'm probably neurodivergent," Sam says quickly. "Autism or ADHD, or maybe both. In case that, um, makes a difference."

I shake my head, dizzy from the zigs and zags of Sam's confessions. "Um. Not really. I mean, I guess it makes sense?"

He nods. "I think it does. And I'm going to investigate further."

I can't drag my eyes from his beautiful face, and I find myself nodding along with him. "That's good."

"One more thing?" Sam asks softly.

"There's more?"

"If I can offer a little piece of advice? From a guy who didn't get a chance to make up with his grandfather or tell my parents how much I loved them before they died?"

Wincing, because I have an idea of what he's going to say, I sigh. "Go on."

"You can love a person and hate their choices. Family that sucks is still family."

Closing my eyes briefly, I file this away for further reflection. When I open them again, I can't stop my grin. Sam is totally rocking a soaking wet white shirt, like the best ever mashup of Colin Firth's Darcy and Cavill's Geralt. "You don't suck, Samuel Bedd, but I love you anyway."

He laughs, his face breaking open like the sun breaking through the clouds overhead. "Thank god. I was afraid I was going to catch pneumonia for nothing."

"You know science has debunked that notion a hundred times over, right?" Hooking my arm through his, I lead him into the storage shed, where I've got a microfiber towel tucked into my bag.

"Yeah, but I still like the idea of you nursing me back to health like in some Jane Austen novel."

While I hand him the towel, something on my phone catches my eye. It's lit up, and my YouTube channel is up on the screen. When I get closer, the donkey's head appears again, but it's live, not playing from the video I took earlier.

I know this, not just because it matches the movement of the donkey across the way, but because the record button is red.

"Oh, shit."

SAM

Gran: Dear Sam,

Gran: I don't know if you know this, but your beautiful declaration of love for Diane was cast out on the internet.

Gran: (I hope she doesn't want us to call her Didi because that name doesn't seem to fit her.)

Gran: When I called Molly to ask if she saw it, she told me that anyone who subscribes to Seeds of Change may have received an alert the way I did, so a few others may have seen it too.

Gran: I hope you'll both join us for Sunday dinner so we can celebrate the fact that you both got your heads out of your behinds and admitted that you love each other.

Gran: Love,

Gran: Your grandmother,

Gran: Ethel

Gran: P.S. I hope you know that I know
that you can't get pneumonia from
standing out in the rain. That's just silly.

My grandmother isn't the only one to text me after Diane accidentally broadcast our conversation live on her channel. Over the next few hours, each of my siblings checks in, except for my sister, which is kind of weird. Even Jackson messages. It's so full of acronyms I have no idea what it says, but it's something.

Come to think of it, I've been getting weird twin vibes the whole afternoon, but when Colleen finally gets back to me, she apologizes and says that her phone died during the annual Fork Lick teacher trip to the city.

For better or for worse, all of Diane's subscribers now know her real identity as well as the fact that we're in love, and in true internet fashion, they all seem to have an opinion about it. Once we get to my new apartment, I manage to tear Diane's phone out of her hand and distract her with kisses that promise more.

After I make sure said phone is powered off, that is.

CHAPTER 24
DIANE

IT IS *SO* MUCH MORE FUN TO HAVE SEX WITH SAM WHEN WE don't have to worry about making noise. We do have to make sure Gomer's occupied, and I'm a little worried that he's going to gain weight with the number of treats he's getting, but now that Sam and I can touch each other as much as we want to, whenever we want to, I can't seem to stop.

We both take Friday off, which includes powering down all devices, and spend the day in bed, only emerging to throw together snacks from Sam's pantry and refrigerator and to take Gomer out. In fact, when we walk through the adorable town of Climax hand in hand, it feels like a dream come true.

Only two things dampen my mood as Friday rolls into Saturday, and both of them have to do with Sam's words to me yesterday. Even though I know he's right, just the thought of contacting my parents and trying to have a relationship with them without getting dragged into their ridiculous lifestyle makes me anxious and exhausted. It's not like they were abusive or anything, but our values are so different it's hard to believe we share the same DNA.

The idea of buying Kaaterskill Orchards is nagging at me too. On the one hand, I may be able to afford it, assuming that the ornithological people are able to stop the development of the property. But I can't quite get to the place where I feel that I should. It still feels too selfish.

When we do turn our phones back on because Sam is worried about Colleen's whereabouts, I do a good job of ignoring the comments on social media. But when I see three voicemails from the realtor representing the orchard property, I can't press play fast enough.

Maybe I do want that property after all.

"Hello Ms. McCarthy, I just wanted to let you know that there's been a change in status to the property on Lot ZXT485. The original buyer dropped out, so if you are still interested in tendering an offer, please contact me as soon as possible."

Suppressing a squeal, I press play for the next message.

"Hi Ms. McCarthy—or should I say Ms. Mayer? I'm not sure. Anyway, I'm calling to let you know that there's been a change in the zoning for Lot ZXT485. Not only is it no longer approved for high-density development, it appears that the orchard may have to remain intact and be maintained due to some ridiculous Bureau of Wildlife claim. Anyway, if you're still interested, please call me."

All I want is to call her and scream, "Yes, I want it!" but I make myself press play for her final message.

"Me again, Ms. McCarthy Mayer. I just wanted to let you know that we have a cash buyer, and the seller has approved the sale, so Lot ZXT485 is no longer available. Have a nice day."

Feeling like I just took the shortest and steepest roller coaster ride ever, adrenaline drains from my body as I sink onto the couch, barely noticing when Gomer noses under my hand. Petting him calms my heart rate enough that I notice there's another voicemail message, this one from an unfamiliar Manhattan area code.

When I press play, the recorded voice is a familiar one. "Didi, it's Seth. Heard you've been tearing it up on social media. Gimme a call, okay?" He then rattles off a number and ends the call.

My eldest brother never was one for chatting, but this is terse even for him. Figuring that if I don't call him, some PR firm my parents hire to mitigate whatever blowback they might get from yesterday's viral video will be next, I punch in the number.

May as well get this reconnection thing over with.

Expecting to have to go through an executive assistant to get to my CFO brother or, at the very least, have my call screened, I'm surprised when Seth answers on the first ring. "Hey, squirt, how the hell are you?"

My heart squeezes at the nickname. There are six years between us, and I idolized my big brother growing up. Hearing his voice makes me realize that Sam may be right. Maybe cutting myself off from my family has its downsides.

"I'm pretty good, considering."

"I've missed you, you know." There's real fondness in his tone, even as he cuts to the chase. "It was good to see your squishy face, even if it was on video. Your channel's pretty cool too. Cheryl and I went down a bit of a rabbit hole watching it yesterday."

"How is Cheryl?" Remembering that I actually like his

wife, I listen as he fills me in on his family's news—milestones their three kids have hit, Cheryl's job at Planned Parenthood, their new kitten.

"And Mom and Dad? They doing okay?"

"They're pretty much the same. Dad's stepping back a bit so they can travel." He clears his throat, and I hear what sounds like a door closing. "Which means I've been able to make some changes."

"Changes?"

My brother worked his way up the investment firm my father established, starting in whatever the financial version of a mailroom is. "Oh, just diversifying the portfolio. In particular, moving money away from dinosaurs like Mayer-SynAgro and rolling into green energy. Things like that."

Before I can ask why, he adds, "Oh, and I bought Nana and Pop's orchard yesterday. Got lucky. Some bird nuts swooped in with a sighting of some rare woodpecker, so I got it for a song. Ha-ha, no pun intended."

Heart in my throat, I whisper, "What are you going to do with it?"

"I dunno. You want it?"

CHAPTER 25
DIANE

WE EMERGE FROM OUR SEX FEST TO HELP OUT AT BERRY picking, followed by the cooking of Sunday dinner. As much as I'm grateful to have reconnected with my brother, which I'm determined to keep up, I still feel like I belong with the Bedds, even though—or perhaps because—I've witnessed some of their struggles. From financial challenges to relationships that needed mending, I've watched Sam and his siblings and grandmother work through it all.

I'm sure we'll have more to come, and I'm here for it.

Tonight, however, we're celebrating. No one seems surprised that Samuel was able to talk me into returning. Perhaps because they watched him do it. No one seems to give two hoots whether I'm really Diane or Didi, McCarthy or Mayer. When asked going forward, I think I'll just say she's all me. I can't change the fact that I was raised with the advantages of the top one percent, but I can and I do choose to live more lightly on this earth. For instance, I can avoid buying a whole new wardrobe by keeping the one I already have, even if my clothes were ridiculously expensive to begin with.

In addition to our newly committed romance, Sam and I have a lot of other news to share. Once we're all seated at the table, I clink a spoon to my glass to get everyone's attention.

"Does that mean I get to kiss my woman?" Ethan yells.

Colleen throws a napkin at him before he and Lia can lock lips. "This isn't a wedding, dumbass."

Her tone is a little sharp, but I can hardly blame her. It might be tough to watch every brother within spitting distance find love one after the other. "Sorry about that," I say. "I just wanted to share our news while we're all here."

"Are you pregnant?" Gran asks, her hands clasped under her chin.

My face heats so fast I have to down a gulp of ice water. I guess that means Gran knows what we've been up to. "No, ma'am. I think we'll wait on that."

"Don't wait too long," Ethel says, pointing a finger at each of her grandkids in turn. "I'm not getting any younger over here."

"Hear, hear!" Molly's dad calls out from the other end of the table. "I vote for grandkids, not just granddogs."

"Anyway," Sam says over the chorus of groans. "Our news has to do with farming."

"That's no fun," Ethan says. "That's all we ever talk about."

"I think it's pretty darn fun," I say. "I didn't get to grow up on my grandparents' farm, but I loved the time I did spend there. And thanks to Samuel, their heirloom orchard is not only going to remain intact, it's back in the family."

Everyone raises their glasses in congratulation, and then I tell the story of how Samuel identified the Red-headed Woodpecker and rallied the Cornell professors behind saving the orchard.

"To be fair, they rallied me. Or called me on the phone and told me exactly what was going to happen."

He goes on to explain that professors in both the Cornell Lab of Ornithology and School of Agriculture have grants at the ready, which they're salivating to employ at Kaaterskill Orchards.

"Where did that name come from?" Molly asks.

"Kaaterskill is the Dutch word for Big Cat Creek, so the Catskill mountains are named for both the mountain lions and creeks that run through the range. My grandmother was Dutch, so she came up with the name.

"This all means," I continue, "that the new owner of the orchard will receive a regular infusion of cash to help manage and care for the trees. All we have to do is give the Cornell teams access whenever they want it."

"You're saying we," Lia notes. "Does that mean you?"

My smile is wide. "It does. It's not official yet, but it turns out that my brother picked up the property when the zoning changed and the price dropped. He offered it to me last night."

"As long as she starts talking to her family again," Sam adds, with a kiss on the cheek.

"Which I'm trying to see as a good thing."

"It is a good thing, sweetheart," Ethel says. "Family is family."

"Will you live there?" Colleen asks. "What about Sam's job?"

"Actually, I think we're going to live at Sam's new apartment in Climax. It'll be more convenient for both of us. I'll move my nonprofit into the orchard's farmhouse.

It'll provide housing for the grad students studying the woodpeckers and apples too."

"This all sounds great," Alex says.

"We're pretty happy," I say, feeling the grin that's been on my face for the past two days appear yet again.

When I raise a brow at Sam, he nods solemnly. "I have more to share. Good news and bad news. Well, more of a clarification than bad news, I guess."

"I usually say good news first, but now I'm intrigued," Ethan says. "What have you got to clarify?"

Sam takes in a breath, and I take his hand and squeeze in support. "I know you all watched me say it on Diane's channel, but I owe the farm about fifty grand. Plus interest."

Lia tips her head to the side. "So that loan marked personal was to you?"

Sam nods, lips pressed together. "Grandad told me the money he gave me to pay for my rent and other expenses not covered by my scholarships at school was a gift. But from what Lia told me, and the dates on a couple of the refis, he just further mortgaged the farm to get it. So, I'm paying it back." He slides a check across the table to Ethan. "This is the first installment."

Ethan holds up a hand. "No matter where he got it, that money was a gift. You don't have to pay it back."

"I do," Sam says, his tone adamant but not angry. "I would've taken out a student loan, so I'm just paying the farm back instead of the government."

Ethan opens his mouth to argue, but Sam stops him. "I want to do this Ethan. It's important to me."

Hands up, Ethan nods, and Lia takes the check.

"Smart woman," Sam says with a grin. Maybe I only

imagine it because I know how much this secret debt has weighed on him, but I swear he sits up taller as he reaches for his fork and stuffs a bite of meatloaf in his mouth.

We all eat in silence for a few moments until Alex says, "Hey, wasn't there also good news? Or was that the good news? I'm confused."

"Right. I almost forgot." Sam wipes his mouth with his napkin, and then pulls a folded piece of paper out of his breast pocket. "I have a proposal for a way to create a buffer field between the soy crop and Gran's expanded vegetable garden."

He slides the paper to Ethan too, but this time Ethan takes it with interest and begins to read.

"Are you going to share with the rest of the class?" Colleen asks.

"Uh, I'm not sure what this means exactly," Ethan says. "So maybe Sam should."

"After talking to the ag school guy who has the grant to study heirloom apples, I did a little calling around to some of my old professors. One of them connected me with a woman studying pesticides. She'd be interested in a ten-year agreement where she pays you to let her experiment on a few acres with pesticides and herbicides that are nonpoisonous."

"But what if they don't work? I'll be out a year's crop," Ethan says.

"That's the beauty of it. Part of her grant covers loss. So she'll reimburse you for any crop damage or reductions."

"Wow," Lia says. "That'd be essentially guaranteed income."

After a long moment where Ethan turns to her and

they engage in some sort of silent communication, Ethan asks, "Can we call a farm meeting real quick?"

"I propose we do," Alex says.

"I second," Colleen says.

"What about Jackson?" Sam asks.

Lia looks up and counts silently on her fingers. "You have a quorum without him."

"A quorum?" Alex asks.

Ethan, Sam and Colleen join him, sticking out their pinky fingers like they're at an English tea and piping the word *quorum* in the worst set of English accents I've ever heard.

Ethan raises his beer glass. "Then I propose we accept Sam's proposal!"

Lia rolls her eyes before looking over at me. "You sure you want to join this nutty crowd?"

"All right, all right," Alex calls out. "I second."

Lia grins. "All in favor, say aye."

The room is filled with a chorus of them.

CHAPTER 26
SAM

I CAN'T REMEMBER THE LAST TIME I ENJOYED A SUNDAY dinner so much, but the second the big hand on the dining room clock hits eleven, Gran jumps up.

"It's almost eight o'clock. I can't miss my show. We'll have to clean up afterwards."

She hustles into the den, Molly on her heels, asking, "Who do you think is going to be eliminated this week?"

"I hope the handsome one makes the top ten," Gran says, a little too breathlessly.

"I think it'll be the guy from Boston," Lia says with an uncharacteristic giggle. "He kind of fell apart last week."

"Do you know what they're talking about?" I ask Diane as I stack plates, figuring I'll do the dishes.

She cranes her head through the doorway so she can see the TV before turning back. "It's that new reality cooking show, *Yes, Chef!* Ethel's obsessed with it."

Colleen takes the plates from me and heads for the kitchen. "You're not a fan, I take it?" I ask, following her with an armful of glasses.

"Nope," my twin says, popping the ending *p* of the word aggressively.

When I return to the dining room to pick up more dirty dishes, Diane is leaning in the doorway, watching the TV from across the hall. Crossing to stand next to her, I watch as the lineup of contestants is introduced. I give her a kiss on the cheek and then a swat on the bum. "Go on and join them. I'm not threatened by hot chefs, because I know you're coming home with me."

She turns, twining her arms around my neck and leaning in to whisper in my ear. "Did you fill up the ice trays before we left the apartment?"

"You know I did," I whisper. "And have I got plans for you."

Ready for more of Bedd Fellows Farm?
Up next is ***Bringing Home the Bacon*** by Erin Mallon.
Everyone thinks Colleen's the sweetest member of the
family, until she falls for a sizzlin' hot chef…

Want more of Sam and Diane? Subscribe at karengrey.com
to access an exclusive bonus epilogue!

FARM 2 FORKING SERIES

Bedd Fellows Farm is in trouble. Grandad bequeathed the five Bedd siblings a heap of debt, along with a troublesome sheep, and they're all too stubborn to accept the help they need to dig their way out of the compost pile.

Join authors Lainey Davis, Liz Alden, Karen Grey, Erin Mallon, and Ember Leigh as they share un-baa-lievable tales of love, laughter, and sexy shenanigans, all set in the bucolic fictional town of Fork Lick, New York.

Meddling grandmas, nosy neighbors, and boinking abound in these steamy romantic comedies.

Since You've Bean Gone by Lainey Davis
Butter You Up by Liz Alden
For Fork's Sake by Karen Grey
Bringing Home the Bacon by Erin Mallon
A Fork in the Road by Ember Leigh

MORE FROM THE AUTHORS

Catch up with the Bedds' neighbors in the Planted and Plowed series by Lainey Davis. Asher Thorne is the hero of Sappy Go Lucky.

Take your romcoms with a side of wanderlust. Kit gets his own story in the upcoming Anywhere But Here series by Liz Alden. In the meantime, check out Aged Like Fine Wine, where four best friends explore Europe and love after forty!

Stayed tuned for a new small town romcom series coming soon from Karen Grey, set down the road from Fork Lick and kicking off with single dad Ben's story! In the meantime, check out her nostalgic romance at karen-grey.com.

As a girl with four brothers, Colleen Bedd knows what it's like to be "one of the guys." For more strong heroines who aren't afraid to go head-to-head with their fellas, dive into The Natural History Series by Erin Mallon.

Jackson's leading lady hails from Bayshore, a small, lakeside Ohio town that sets the stage for Ember's other rom-coms. Visit Bayshore now to meet the Daly brothers, and to get ready for the next series launching soon.

ACKNOWLEDGMENTS

I could not have made my way out of the 20th century and into writing contemporary romance without my Farm 2 Forking co-conspirators. Dreaming up Fork Lick, NY and its denizens was not only a blast, but ego- and drama-free thanks to co-writers Liz Alden, Lainey Davis, Ember Leigh and Erin Mallon.

Thanks to Jax Garden for an insightful edit, and to Elizabeth Taylor for the helpful beta read.

Thanks to the real life MT Bottles (@mtbottlescomedy on Instagram), who is responsible for my own trivia night addiction. If you're ever in Wilmington, NC please check out his comedy shows!

I have to shout out the Cornell Lab of Ornithology. If you're at all interested in birds, download the Merlin app now (be forewarned, it will not call you if you happen upon an endangered species)!

Finally, thanks to you, dear reader. I hope you've enjoyed getting to know Sam and Diane and the rest of Fork Lick as much as we've loved telling their stories, because we couldn't do it without you.

ALSO BY KAREN GREY

<u>Carolina Classics Series</u>

You Get What You Give

Hold On To Me

I Want It That Way

When I Come Around

<u>Boston Classics Series</u>

What I'm Looking For

Forget About Me

You Spin Me

Child of Mine

ABOUT THE AUTHOR

KAREN GREY is a *USA Today* bestselling and award-winning author of vintage romantic comedies with smart heroines and hunky heroes. Drawing on a long career as a performer, her retro 80's and 90's romances are populated with characters working both on- and off-stage in theater, TV and film. When not reading or writing, she's lounging at the beach or hiking in the mountains. Or dreaming about both with an IPA in hand and a dog or a cat nearby.

(Author photo: Celestial Studios)

For the latest news and bonus materials, join her free VIP club at: followkarengrey.com

facebook.com/karengreyauthor

instagram.com/karengreyauthor

goodreads.com/karen_grey

bookbub.com/profile/karen-grey

tiktok.com/@karengreyauthor